I0598868

COLUMBUS: WINTER
Project Columbus, Book 4

By J.C. Rainier

Columbus: Winter
Project Columbus, Book 4
Copyright © 2013 by J.C. Rainier
Published: 26 November 2013
ISBN: 978-1-939817-07-5
Publisher: Oakenbrand Press

In conjuction with Oakenbrand Press.

Currently Available by J.C. Rainier:

Columbus: Flight

Columbus: Ashes

Columbus: Demeter

Coming April 2014:

Columbus: Mercy

Other Projects by J.C. Rainier:

The Sorcerers - Web Comic by J.C. Rainier and A. Kochetova –
http://sorcerers.manyhatsonline.com

Please follow J. C. on Facebook or Twitter (@JCRainier), or check **http://jcrainier.com** periodically for blog updates and sneak previews of the Project Columbus series.

>BEGIN PLAYBACK|

CONCORDIA

DUM VITA EST

SPES EST

Per Defectum Unitate

Connor Hammond
28 Mar, 1 year after landing (yal), late
morning
Western coast of Raphael Island
>|

Instinct made Connor turn his head as a wave crashed into the jagged rock spit. Instinct that was conspicuously lacking when he made the decision to crawl onto it. Salt water washed over his head, dislodging a week's worth of sand from his shaggy, curled locks. His eyelids shut in an instant, keeping the coarse grit from flowing down into his eyes. The tips of his fingers trembled even as they clutched at the sharp stones. He crept forward, keeping in a low crouch. The further away from shore he got, the more he realized how rapidly the tide was rising.

That will only make this easier in the end, he thought, fighting back his fear.

Connor glanced back at the shore. Three men scrambled for footholds on the spit, closing in on him from the glittering white strand of beach far behind. His heart pounded as his nerves tingled. He didn't want the strangers to put themselves in peril, but it was necessary. If they got too close to him, the consequences would be dire. He moved forward, slowly picking the safest path along the increasingly treacherous and narrow finger of land. The seas swelled and churned ahead of the young man. He paused for just a second at the thought of being soaked in the salty water, then laughed at how dumb it was to worry about something so trivial. After all, he was about to die. His only concern was to go far enough out that he wouldn't be followed, but stay close enough to shore that his pursuers would still be able to hear him out.

His foot slipped, splitting the tattered remnants of his shoe open. Pain shot through his ankle as it turned under him. Flailing for a hand hold, he tumbled backward, hitting the ground hard. The pain as his head slapped the rock shot through him with furious intensity, and he swallowed a lungful of sea water as he started to curse. His vision blurred; whether from the blow to his skull or from the rinse of sea water, he couldn't tell. Connor struggled to sit up and wiped away the stinging water from his face. His pursuers were closing the gap, and seemed motivated by his fall.

"Stay back!" he shouted. They continued undeterred. He repeated his warning, again to no avail.

Connor struggled to his feet, the nerves in his ankle and head taking turns with searing warnings of the damage done. He pressed his fingers to the back of his head and drew them away, tinted pink with diluted blood. Connor crouched again and moved two steps to the side, to the brink of the roiling surf.

"Are you crazy? Get away from there! You're going to get yourself killed!" The shout was barely audible over the thundering waves.

"Stay back!" he repeated.

The men approached slowly, one with his hand extended in front of him, as if the simple pleading gesture would bring Connor to his senses and compel him to follow them. For a moment he wanted to give in. He yearned to surrender to the selfish voice inside and ignore the consequences in exchange for a solid meal and restful night's sleep. Connor could see the smoke rise from the distant hill that marked the final destination for the survivors. For weeks he and his comrades had journeyed through jungle and sand, searching for the settlement in a desperate last bid for help. Only Connor seemed to see the folly for what it was.

"Come on, kid," the leader shouted as he crept closer. "It ain't safe out here. Supertide's gonna come in and wipe us all off these rocks in a couple of minutes. I don't want you to drowning out here or getting smashed on the rocks."

Connor rose up slowly, trembling. "Stay back or I'll kill you."

"Y'ain't got no weapons, kid. Now come on back and we'll talk 'bout whatever's eating you up."

"No, you don't understand! I'll kill you if you get near me. If you touch me, or get too close to me, you're as good as dead."

"No need to threaten me. I'm here to help you."

"Then help me, but don't come any closer," he retorted, his voice starting to become hoarse from powering over the waves.

"I can't help you if you won't let me get near you, kid."

"Yes, you can. Just listen to me."

The men paused, still about ten or fifteen feet away. "Alright, I'm listening."

Good. Still far enough away.

"They're coming. A whole bunch of them are coming your way. And you have to stop them. No matter what you say, you have to turn them away."

"Who's coming?"

"Survivors. You can't let them in, though. You can't let them near you. You can't let them in your camp, or you'll all die."

The leader's face twisted in shock. "They armed?"

"Yeah, but they're not here to fight. They just want to join your people, but you can't let them. You'll die."

The shock melted away and was replaced by confusion as the three men exchanged glances. "How are they gonna kill us if they ain't here to fight?"

Connor opened his mouth to explain the terrible truth, but before he could utter a word, he was knocked off his feet by a powerful wave, crashing into the spit with irresistible, raw energy. Time seemed to slow as he fell, and Connor wondered if the men from Captain Kimura's village would heed his warning, even as he failed to explain the situation. His shoulder impacted the rocky breakwater a moment before the current dragged him out into the open water.

"Jesus," Nick cursed, still unable to comprehend what had unfolded before his eyes. The tips of his fingers tingled, and his feet were rooted firmly in the sand despite his urge to pace about.

Martin just swore, as he had since the tide had pulled the young stranger out to sea. The steady stream of expletives was broken only long enough for him to cycle new breaths. Mike sat on the soft, wet sand as soon as they had made their way off the rocky spit.

Only a few minutes earlier, the supertide had swallowed up the entire beach, leaving them stranded on a high point, surrounded completely by water. It had been just barely large enough for Nick and his companions to ride out the rapidly rising and retreating tide.

"Jesus, Martin, why the hell'd you drag us out there?" Nick blurted. "We could have been killed, just like that kid."

"I didn't think it'd go that far." Martin pulled his graying hair back from his forehead, flattening the wrinkles on his sun-scorched brow. "What the hell was his problem?"

Nick shook his head. He looked down at his fingers, which were trembling. This was the second time he had watched someone die. But with Lon Carney, it was different. Carney was a murderer, a desperado. This stranger was desperate alright, but he had done no wrong. The wild look in his eyes haunted Nick, even after his body had been dragged to its watery grave.

"He was going on about something, but I couldn't hear. Did you understand any of it?"

Martin grumbled and shrugged. "No. The kid was just some fucked up lunatic. Saying he was going to kill me if I touched him, that we're all dead anyway, some other nonsense shit like that. I've heard that kind of shit before. Sounded a bit like Carney to me. Or Stillmark, just before he ate his own bullet."

"Dude," Nick interrupted, cringing with shame for his vulgar companion's disregard of the dead. "Go easy on him. Yeah, he was disturbed, but he didn't need to go out there. We could have helped him."

"Like your dad helped Maria?" Martin sneered. He snorted deeply through his nose and spat the resulting glob of mucous on the ground. "I ain't waiting for that little situation to get better. No, your daddy ain't no shrink, Nick. If that boy was rattled enough to go out there and try and kill himself, he's better off."

Nick felt his temper flare. He narrowed his eyes as he brought his caustic gaze to bear on Martin. The older man's callousness was one of the reasons that Nick couldn't wait for the completion of his own fishing canoe. For almost a year he had been paired with Martin. Most days Nick was able to ignore or tolerate the man. Others he was unbearable or even abusive.

"Martin's right," Mike added quietly.

Nick glanced over at the third member of the crew, who now stared almost blankly out at the ocean horizon. He had been assigned to their canoe for three months now. Mike was a likeable, albeit quiet, man. At nineteen, he was a little younger than Nick. Normally he had an optimistic view on things, so his agreement with Martin took Nick by surprise.

"What?" he gasped.

"Think about it. The supertide's coming in. He sees us and bolts onto the rocks. He keeps going even when we tell him to stop. I mean, if he just didn't want us to get near him, why run onto the rocks? Why not just run out into the jungle?"

"Because of the jaguars, maybe?"

Mike shook his head. "Jaguar *might* get him. But going out there with the water coming in like that? It's like he wanted to die."

"Fuckin' nutjob," Martin muttered.

Nick sighed, resigning himself to the fact that they were probably right. The spit was dangerous on a good day, which is why most fishermen avoided it. They were lucky to get out with their own lives. Nick walked away from his companions and headed for their canoe. The bow line was slack, resting in the sand. The tide had flowed out far enough that their boat was completely beached. They would have to carry the boat down to the water to shove off and make way for home.

"You going to be ok?" Mike asked as Nick busied himself with untying their line.

"Yeah," he shrugged.

"C'mon, you two," Martin growled. "We ain't got time to cry over this kid. We're behind now, and I don't want to go home empty handed today."

Nope. Only empty hearted.

* * *

Karen Daniels
Late in the afternoon
>|

Jack was sprinting down the beach at full speed. This was unusual, Karen noted. In the year that she had known him, she had only seen him run once, and then he had a long-tusked boar hot on his heels. In this case he was not being pursued, and his pistol rested in its holster. He clearly had something important to report, and this time that something didn't have a desire to tear him to shreds.

Karen gathered her two closest lieutenants—an honorific title, rather than the actual rank, last held by the late Matt Marsolek—and waited for Jack's return.

Mina passed the time by going through a series of poses. Before life on Demeter, Mina had a career as a yoga instructor. While that particular career was not useful on Demeter, she had proven to have energy, strength, and determination to spare. Karen relied on the young, slender woman for her ability to keep the column of survivors in line and on task, and she had a knack for finding edible plants out in the jungle.

Jacob, the other lieutenant, whittled away at a small stick. He loved to carve native vegetation in his spare time, but had only truly mastered one item: sharpened stakes. Besides making hazardous kindling, he had his uses. Most notably, this came in the form of pest control. It just happened that the majority of fauna that fell into this category were dangerous enough to kill humans. Jacob's keen eye, when paired with a rifle, meant sure death to predators like the jaguar. As the survivors were essentially a column of fresh meat, Jacob was often quite busy.

Jack was Karen's right hand man. Nearly killed in the wreck of pod four, he battled his way back to health, only to fall ill with the jungle plague. He, like Karen, nearly died of the ailment. But in the words of the late Brett Wu, "He just willed himself back to health." Jack was the rock that the survivors clung to. He was what kept them from slipping back into the despair and chaos that had nearly torn apart the Lake Raphael encampment. And it was his approval of this mission that swayed the people, bringing them to abandon Lake Raphael and follow Karen along the coast. They needed help, and if the settlement even still existed, they would be the only ones that could help.

Suddenly Karen realized that Jack wasn't alone on the glittering white strand. Two more men lagged behind him, though their pace was more of a brisk jog than Jack's headlong sprint. He easily closed the gap and presented himself to Karen for his report. He smiled, though he panted from being out of breath. Jack saluted; Karen had learned months earlier to ignore the childish dig. She was the only one of *Raphael's* crew members left among the ragged band. Command structure had long ago been washed away. People still listened to and respected Karen, but her Air Force rank was now a forgotten, meaningless fact.

"It's here?" she asked hopefully.

Jack nodded. He managed enough breath to gasp, "A little over a mile from here."

"You met with them? Can they help us?"

He nodded again.

The two strangers caught up and came to a stop only a few feet away. Their eyes were wide, and one's jaw almost hit the floor. The leader appeared to be a rather short, slender man with unkempt hair and a wild beard. He wore an M9 on his hip, though it was oddly disproportionate on him. Karen was surprised to see a familiar face in the other man, though it took a moment to recognize him through the beard.

"Seth? Seth Leight?" she said, mouth agape. "You're still alive?"

"K-Karen," he stuttered. "I… I thought you were dead. The last time I heard from Marsolek on the radio, you…"

He took a step toward her, his eyes scrutinizing her from head to toe.

"I almost was. Barely pulled through. Marsolek wasn't so lucky. The disease took him."

Seth nodded. "How long ago?"

"Nine months."

The shorter man cleared his throat. "I assume you're in charge, then?"

Karen turned her attention to him and nodded. "Tech Sergeant Karen Daniels, USAF. Formerly of the sleeper ship *Raphael*. If you'll pardon us, we don't use my rank anymore."

"Nor mine," Seth interrupted.

Seth's companion shot him a quick glance, then continued. "I'm Chief James Vandemark of Camp Eight."

Karen paused, puzzled at the title he had used in reference to himself. "Chief?"

James nodded. "It's a little humor. A play on being stranded on this island. It started one night during a village meeting and kind of snowballed from there."

"Ah, I see. So what's your real title then?"

"Chief," he replied. His voice was dead serious, and she suddenly realized that what had started as a joke had morphed into their reality.

"Uh, alright." Karen shifted uncomfortably and cleared her throat. "As you can see, we've all come a long way. I'm sure you've figured out this isn't a social visit, either."

"You need our help."

"Yes."

"Are you offering help in return?"

Karen looked behind her at the remaining colonists under her care. When Lake Raphael had formed as a collection point for crashed pods on the east side of the mountain range, almost six hundred people lived there. Now Karen had only a hundred fifty-two. Most were huddled in family or social cliques underneath the towering salt palms, though a few had ventured closer, hoping to catch a bit of the exchange between Karen and the leaders of the place they hoped to call home.

"We can only offer you ourselves. We have nothing else left. Need foragers or fishermen? We can help with that. Hands to build structures and hands to care for children, we have that as well."

"Do you have any food?" James asked without any hesitation.

"Enough for today and tomorrow," Mina replied. "But we can get to work earning our keep tomorrow."

James looked carefully around at the gathered crowd. He paced slowly from one side to another, seeming to analyze each person he saw. When he finished analyzing an individual, he appeared to calculate and move on to another. Time ticked away as he did this, and Karen could sense the agitation of her lieutenants as the delay mounted.

"When can I speak with Captain Kimura?" she asked.

The chief stopped dead in his tracks, but did not give Karen any specific regard otherwise. "Captain Kimura is dead."

Karen nodded as she swallowed hard. Her heart sank.

She was the one who made the offer to Lieutenant Marsolek. Shit, did she tell anyone else about the offer?

Karen looked at Seth, pleading with her eyes for some sort of help from him. He just nodded once, then returned to his cold observation of the chief's antics.

"Do you have any ill among your group?" James finally asked, though his tone was almost inhumanly cold.

Don't lie. You'll make things worse when they find out.

"We have two people sick. They're starting to get better at this point."

"They stay on the beach, along with anyone else who has had close contact with them over the past week," James spat back, cutting her off. "They'll only be allowed in the village once our doctor clears them. Also, anyone who has not yet contracted this disease has to stay on the beach as well, again until our doctor clears them."

"Why?" she asked.

"Two reasons. First, because I don't want to put my people at any undue risk. And second, because I said so."

"I... I..." Karen stammered. "Thank you, sir."

"It's chief," James said as he turned away, whistling at Seth to follow him. "Welcome home, Sergeant."

Fractis in Posterum, Act I

Gabrielle Serrano
17 Jul, 1 yal, early morning
Camp Eight
>|

"Mama?" Gabi asked as she rubbed the sands of slumber from her eyes.

She could hear the faint rush of wind over the roof, and Diego let out a soft squeal next to her. Though mostly dark inside their tiny hut, light filtered through the cracks and gaps between logs where the mud used to seal the cracks had washed away. She watched as her tiny brother yawned and stretched his pale arms before settling back to sleep. She then scanned the room, but her mother was nowhere to be found. Nor was any sort of breakfast. Gabi's stomach growled sternly, and she hugged her belly to calm it.

Diego startled at her movement. He opened his eyes, and immediately his lip curled into a pout and he began to cry. Gabi offered her finger to him, which he gripped tenaciously. She tried to soothe him by singing, but his wail only escalated.

"Are you hungry, Diego?" she asked softly.

Waiting for an answer would be pointless. Gabi knew that Diego couldn't talk at all, and he wouldn't be able to for a few years, from what Emilia had told her. Instead she gently scooped him up and cradled him in her arms the way that the adults had taught her. She then carefully stood up and paced around the hut a few times, gently rocking him and admiring his cool, blue eyes.

Gabi loved Diego's eyes. She was a little jealous of them, and every now and then wished that she could trade her brown eyes for blue ones just like his. She never did understand why her mother hated Diego's eyes, or why her mother said they made her cry when she looked into them.

At the same time, Gabi was thankful that she had almond skin, unlike her brother. She had seen enough of the white-skinned colonists come home with painful sunburns to know that, though it set her apart somewhat, Bravo's effects were not going to be as harsh on her. She also felt sorry that her brother would have to deal with sunburns when he was older.

Her stomach grumbled again, reminding her that food would have to come sooner than later. She turned to leave the hut when the storm curtain pulled back.

"Mama?" she asked the dark silhouette ringed by blinding daylight.

"Morning, Gabi." The soft female voice was not her mother's. Jeanette stepped inside the hut, much to Gabi's surprise and excitement. It had been some time since any of the Vandemarks had visited. Or anyone else, for that matter.

Two months earlier, over a hundred new people had come to Camp Eight from far off, and the people of the village had been working extra hard to welcome them and make them feel at home. Gabi had wanted to meet these strangers, but she had to help her mother care for Diego, and she had been warned by her mother that she'd just get in the way and cause trouble. Only on the rare occasion that Gabi's mother let her go to school did she see anyone, and even then she found it impossible to make friends with the new kids, as Marya had beaten her to it.

As Gabi's eyes adjusted to the shift in light she could see a soft, somber smile on Jeanette's face. It was a look that she wore when her mind was far away. Jeanette's pants were streaked with caked mud, and her shirt had picked up a dusty brown sheen. It didn't look like she had washed them in a couple days. "How's Diego?" she asked as she stepped closer.

"He's a cranky pants. I think he's hungry."

Jeanette bit her lip and nodded. "C'mon, let's get you guys something to eat."

"Alright," Gabi chirped cheerfully. "Can you carry him? He makes my arms tired."

"Of course, sweetie."

Jeanette took Diego from her. Gabi felt at once as if she could leap over the buildings in the village. She began to skip about, quickly pulling aside the storm curtain as they left, cheering about her impending breakfast. She asked Jeanette if there were eggs this morning, and bragged about how many pepperines she could eat. After jabbering nonstop for almost four minutes, asking a half dozen questions without answer, Gabi began to wonder if Jeanette was upset.

As they queued in line for breakfast at the village square, she timidly whispered, "Are you mad at me?"

"Huh?" Jeanette's eyebrows knitted together in confusion for a moment. "No, no, not at all, honey."

Gabi looked around for her mother, certain that she would be around for Diego's feeding. She couldn't find her in the crowd, but she did see a lot of the adults turn away as soon as her eyes caught theirs.

"Where's Mama?"

"Don't worry about that, dear. Have some breakfast."

"What about Diego? He doesn't have any teeth yet!"

"I know. Don't worry."

Gabi scrunched her nose and faced forward again, and she felt a hint of disappointment at Jeanette's deflection. She quickly forgot as the line moved forward and she could catch a glimpse of what was available this morning.

No eggs. She sighed and her shoulders slumped in a dramatic fashion.

"This isn't a very good day, is it?" she asked. Jeanette just looked ahead, not reacting to the question at all. Even when Diego fussed, she barely took notice.

Why won't she talk to me? Gabi felt a greasy knot in the pit of her stomach. She wondered if Jeanette was indeed upset, but hiding it from her. It wouldn't be the first time that an adult had lied to her, and it hurt her every time she found out about another falsehood.

"Hey Gabi," Marya called to her. She folded her dingy arms across her chest as she came face to face with Gabi. She had a sneer on her face, something that seemed perpetual whenever she wasn't playing.

"What?" Gabi shot back. She had no patience with the older girl. It would shame Gabi to admit it, but she secretly dreamed about Marya being dragged into the jungle by a pack of jaguars.

"Who ya gonna stay with now, huh?"

Jeanette suddenly no longer seemed lost in her thoughts, and her thousand mile stare was gone. "Not now, Marya," she said sternly.

"Huh?" Gabi asked, confused.

"I said who you gonna stay with?"

"Marya. Go away, *now*," Jeanette warned. Gabi picked up on a hint of anger in her tone, and at once she instinctively froze in place, rigid as a board.

"You gonna live with them?" Marya continued, jerking her thumb at Jeanette.

"Marya. Last warning. Go away." Jeanette stepped out of line, using her body as a barrier between the two girls.

Marya leaned out to the side, apparently undeterred by Jeanette's stern warning. "What about Diego? Is he going with you? Are you his new mommy?"

"His new what?" Gabi gasped, horrified and confused.

Why would I be Diego's mommy? Why wouldn't Mama?

Jeanette's hand flew through the air in a blur. There was a sickening smack, and Marya's head twisted to the side from the open-handed blow. "You horrible little shit," she growled. "Go home *now*."

Marya cupped her hand over her eye and almost instantly burst into tears. She staggered off toward her home. Diego cried out in fright. Gabi stood fast, overwhelmed both with fear of Jeanette and her mounting confusion. Her questions repeated over and over in her head.

"Mama?" Gabi asked quietly. Her lip trembled, though she wasn't sure why. Something inside her cried out that something terrible was going on.

"Oh, sweetie," Jeanette knelt in front of Gabi, still cradling Diego in one arm. A single tear rolled down her cheek. "Oh, sweetie I'm so sorry. This wasn't the way... I..." she seemed to struggle with her words.

"Mama?" Gabi repeated, choking up. Her suspicions were confirmed: something terrible had happened.

"I'm so sorry, Gabi. Your mama is with the angels now."

There were no words. Gabi knew what that meant. Haruka was with the angels. She would never see Haruka again. She would never see her mother again. Her mother was gone, and all she had left was Diego, her tiny, four-month-old brother.

J.C. Rainier

Shit, this is a mess.

"Fuck, Jeannie!" he bellowed.

"Don't yell at me," his wife snapped back. Her eyes glistened with tears, though her pain was matched by her fury. "What the hell else was I supposed to do?"

"I don't know, not tell her that her mom fucking killed herself?"

"I had to tell her something!"

"You were supposed to break it to her easy. You were supposed to tell her that her mother was gone. You weren't supposed to tell her *how* or *why.*"

James shouted an expletive and turned away from his wife. He couldn't bear to look at her. What she had done to Gabi was devastating. Near unforgiveable. The poor girl had a hard enough time on Demeter without the day's events. She woke up this morning blissfully unaware of what Maria Serrano had done. And in a matter of minutes, Jeannie had crushed what little good the girl had left in her life.

She wasn't supposed to know. She didn't need to know.

"She wasn't supposed to find out from Marya," Jeanette pointed out. "How the hell is that my fault?"

James let out a laugh that was twisted by sarcasm and disgust. "How isn't it? You know how Marya and Gabi are together. What the hell were you doing even letting them get that close? Especially on a day like today. And then hitting Marya afterward?"

"Alright, it wasn't my finest moment," she growled.

"No. It wasn't. Not by a long shot."

"But you riding my ass isn't fucking helping, James."

"Neither is telling that poor broken kid that her mother killed herself."

"God damn it," she screamed, tearing at her hair. "I'm sorry. I didn't want to."

"But you did it anyway," he snapped. "So don't tell me you didn't want to. If you don't want to do something like that, you just don't do it. Don't make excuses afterwards."

She clenched her fists and screamed in hatred and anguish. Tears were streaming down her cheeks, and she paced from one wall of the hut and back again, kicking at the dirt as she fumed.

James sighed heavily. He had only had one argument this heated with Jeannie back on Earth. It nearly destroyed their marriage. The venom that they held for each other lingered for weeks. Their children had felt the repercussions, and Kristin had broken down into tears in fear of her parents splitting up. His heart had felt as if a stake of shame and regret had been driven through it at the times, like seeing his then seven year old girl bawling her eyes out. This was somehow worse, fighting over what was to become of this girl who, though not related by blood, had become like family to them.

"Fine," he caved. "What's done is done. I don't know, maybe if we just raise her as our own, she'll forget."

"Oh, you think you're going to get off that easily?" she snarled.

"No. Blame me all you want. Scream at me, tear my head off for all I care. But we need to work out how to help Gabi."

She stared daggers at him for a moment, but then nodded and folded her arms across her chest. "Fine. Say we take in Gabi. What about Diego?"

Diego, he thought. *Diego will be lucky to survive without his mother.*

"We take him in too. It's not like he's going to have better chances with anyone else. None of the other women…" James trailed off, not wanting to finish the sentence.

Jeanette nodded, not wanting to finish it either. Diego was in a tough position. His mother was the only woman who could produce breast milk. Charlotte Bryant, Troy's new wife, was still months away from giving birth. The tiny baby's life rested on whether or not he could stomach boar's milk. And whether anyone in the colony was brave enough to try milking a wild boar.

God, kid… your mom really screwed you, didn't she?

* * *

J.C. Rainier

Messis Pulvis

Darius never had a green thumb. He could keep a cactus alive, but not much else. It hadn't particularly bothered him until now. Not because he had great aspirations of growing a bountiful garden of his own, but because what he saw in the field before him frightened him. It didn't take a degree in agricultural science or a lifetime of tilling fields to know that the short, withered corn stalks rustling in the breeze were not healthy. Ranging from pale green to slightly brown, each spear clung to the parched and cracked ground through roots that desperately needed rain.

The weather in Concordia had not been kind to a number of plants imported from Earth. The corn was one of the more striking visual examples. Darius reached his hand out to touch one of the stalks. It was coarse like sandpaper, and the leaves rustled under the soft touch of his fingers. The ears of corn were clearly underdeveloped, even to his untrained eyes. The orchard trees weren't faring any better; their growth had been ground almost to a halt by the dry weather. Though the orchard wasn't expected to bear fruit for many years to come, the farmers had told Darius that this drought, if survived by the trees, would stunt their production for another year.

Drought. At least the scientists don't think it's going to be like this every year.

Concern had been slowly mounting amongst botanists and farmers alike that perhaps Demeter was not as hospitable as once thought. Speculation in the scientific community had led some to believe that the native life on Demeter required almost no water for survival. Others refuted this, pointing to the Fairweather River as evidence to the contrary. After all, if most life needed only a little water, any low-water plant life found near such a mighty river would surely drown from abundance.

As spring gave way to summer, fear mounted. It had been a long time since it had rained hard enough to soak the soil. Too long in the opinion of many. A comprehensive comparative study was launched to determine how Demeter's flora was faring, and many native plants varieties also appeared to be affected. This led to the determination of drought as being the probable cause of stress to Concordia's agricultural assets, both foreign and domestic. While the revelation eased the minds of the people, it did nothing to assuage Darius's concerns.

J.C. Rainier

"Alright, I've seen enough here. Give me some good news," Darius said, turning to the three farm representatives.

The three men were almost absurdly stereotypical in appearance, bordering on comical. Heavy, dirt caked boots protected their feet, while durable denim and knit cloths wrapped everything above. Their arms were deeply tanned to where their clothing cut off, as were their brows. One minor detail threw off Darius's image of farmers from the Midwest; the conspicuous lack of baseball hats. Only one of the three men wore one. The other two sported hats of woven straw with wide brims, crafted the previous summer from the tough native grasses.

George Kasch, the oldest of the three at forty-two years of age, nodded to the rest and motioned for Darius to follow. As they walked along a narrow foot trail that ran between two fields, he began his report.

"So the corn's screwed for this year. Probably the wheat too. We should have enough seed stock to plant again next year. We've still got millet and sorghum growing. There's a lot of it, too."

Darius grimaced. *Corn and wheat feed a lot of hungry mouths. That's a lot to lose.*

"Enough to feed everyone and the animals?"

"No," George admitted. "But we've got a halfway decent crop of beans going. Most varieties you could think of, too. That will help a ton with feeing the people. Once the harvest is over we might get some fodder out of the stock, too." He pointed out several wide patches still-green plants growing on the flanks of one of the small hills. *Gabriel* dominated the landscape beyond, masking Concordia from their view.

"What about native plants?"

The farmer shrugged. "So so. The pears, onions, and potatoes aren't doing so well. Neither are the greens. Most everything else is at least okay."

Darius stopped in his tracks. "Wait, the potatoes aren't growing?"

"Not real well, no."

"And what about Earth potatoes?" Darius waited for an answer. Without words, volumes were spoken. George exchanged glances with the other representatives. One cleared his throat. "Now wait just a minute. You're now talking about three staple crops failing. I was uncomfortable hearing that two were going to be an issue. Now you're telling me it's three? *And* supplemental crops, too?"

"Look, it's probably going to rain any day now," George said, trying to assure him. "Craig's been charting the weather and he thinks it's going to change in a couple days or so."

"And what if it doesn't? Or what if it does rain, but only as much as last time? What if it all dries up the second it hits the ground?" Another round of silence confirmed his fear.

Then we might starve this winter.

They came to the main road to town. Darius thanked the farmers for their time and effort, and took his leave. As he walked slowly back to his temporary office on *Gabriel*, he weighed a number of scenarios surrounding the likelihood of food shortages. Every ending confirmed one thing.

I need to take action now. Waiting will only make it worse.

J.C. Rainier

"Come again, Governor?"

The corner of Darius's mouth twitched once. He had told Roger numerous times that he didn't have to use his title when talking. It felt somehow empty when the colonists addressed him as "Governor," but it was outright bizarre to hear it from the man he had worked so closely with for years. From the time Darius arrived in Wyoming for training to the moment *Gabriel* touched down, they held the same rank, and sat shoulder to shoulder. Now Darius was governor, and Roger was his liaison. Darius was placed in high regard by the people, but Roger was just the quiet guy with the limp who did the governor's bidding. It all seemed unfair to Darius, and the use of his title only heightened his awareness of the disparity.

"I know it sounds a bit unusual," he replied, making sure to give eye contact to both of the men seated across the table.

"Unusual?" Tom countered. "Unusual doesn't begin to describe it, Darius. You're talking about scrapping all of the construction work that we've done so far this year."

"Not scrap," he corrected. "Place on hold. And it would only affect the unfinished buildings."

"It might as well be scrapping them. If you stop construction on most of those buildings now, they're not going to be standing come next spring. Hell, some of them might not even survive autumn."

Concern was deeply etched on his deputy's face. It was a concern that Darius shared, to which he couldn't afford to give life. The construction of the market square in North Concordia was Darius's pet project, idealized and set in motion during the dying days of the previous summer. But as Bravo blazed overhead, baking the ground relentlessly, he knew that something had to give. Securing more food for the upcoming winter was of far greater importance than construction of shops and apartments.

"If we still have time before the weather turns, we can put people back on those projects. Maybe even shore them up enough to survive the winter. But the reports I'm getting on the harvest aren't pretty."

"Reports?" Tom asked sharply. "I've only seen one. It wasn't great, but we were still okay. When did you get these other reports?"

Darius sighed and rubbed at his shaved scalp. "The latest one was two days ago. I spoke with Kasch, Porter, and Lopez. It's bad, gentlemen. We've got at least three staple crops that we can't count on at all. What's harvested will probably need to be used to plant next season. Fresh greens are also not doing well, which will put a strain on all the other vegetables."

"My God," Roger gasped.

"Three?" Tom echoed. "That's going to severely impact our winter stores."

"That's an understatement, Tom," Darius agreed.

"So are we clearing more farms with the extra labor you've freed up?"

Darius shook his head. "Planting more crops in dried ground isn't going to get us anywhere. I need the townspeople split into four groups. Take most of the men from the construction projects. They're going back on construction, but I have something else in mind."

Tom nodded as he began to scribble notes with a well-worn pencil. "Alright, go ahead."

"First, I want the construction teams to build an irrigation system. Go upriver if you have to, but take four of the portable pumps from the ships' supplies to take the water from the river. Have them make it as extensive as they can. I know we're short on time and materials, but they need to get creative."

"Irrigation? Isn't it a bit late?"

"Better late than never. The second and third groups are going out into the wilderness. Make sure they're armed and have enough supplies. Loan out all the crawlers if you have to. One group needs to collect native fruit and vegetables. As much as possible. The other group I want either hunting or fishing. Again, we need them to bring back as much as possible."

"You're asking for people to get killed out there, Governor," Roger protested. "We shouldn't be picking berries in the middle of reaper bear territory."

"Let me ask you, Roger," Darius responded with no hesitation. "Would you rather be killed quickly by a reaper bear or die slowly of starvation?" He waited for a moment before continuing, making sure that his liaison was thoroughly shocked by the question. "That's what I thought. No one goes alone, got it?"

Roger nodded. Tom continued taking notes. "And the fourth group?"

"Preserving the food. If it's picked from a bush, shot in the forest, or dragged out of the river, I want it in a can, jar, or barrel. We'll measure success by how many cargo pods we fill. Our target is three per ship."

"We only used two pods of rations per ship last winter."

"This isn't going to be as space efficient," Darius replied. "And we don't even have a week's worth of those rations left. If we don't get three per ship at a minimum, we're starving. Remember that when we're filling the quota. Also, I want to start rationing what we've already got. The sooner we start stockpiling, the better."

"Rationing?" Roger complained. "That's not going to make people happy."

"I don't care about happy right now. I care about what will happen this winter." Darius cleared his throat, steeling himself for another unpleasant order. "All current supplies of fruits and vegetables that can be canned are to be processed immediately. Going forward, residents are only allowed two pieces of fruit and two servings of vegetables per person, per day."

"You can't be serious!"

"I can and I am. Now do it!"

Roger shrunk in his chair at the barked command. Darius felt a twinge of regret immediately, as his friend deserved better treatment than such an outburst.

"And what do we tell the people whose homes we stop building because of all of this?" Tom asked.

Darius folded his hands in front of him. "Sorry. See you on the ship this winter."

This could get ugly, Darius thought as he exchanged glances with Roger.

"Please, move away and let the workers through," he urged the small crowd of about two dozen colonists that blocked the base of *Michael's* rear cargo ramp. On the other side of the crowd idled a crawler, its bed full of barrels containing pickled fish and jerked meat.

Shouts of defiance and loud questions mixed together, drowning each other out in a cacophony of chaos. It had only been a few hours since Darius had shot down any immediate possibility of reassigning the construction crews back to work in the town square, but rumor and gossip traveled quickly throughout the populace. Darius knew he couldn't keep the severity of the drought a secret from the small, close-knit townspeople forever, but he had hoped for at least a little more time before having to deal with any backlash. His disappointment grew deeper when he spotted Calvin McLaughlin in the fray.

"Please, let the crawler through," he repeated. "They have work to do."

"We'll move once you agree to talk to us," one man shouted to a chorus of approval.

Well if that's all it is…

"Fine. Tomorrow morning at six. Where would you like to meet?"

"No, Governor. Now. We won't wait."

Again the crowd cheered in response to the man's demands.

"Don't do it," Roger whispered in his ear. "They're all riled up."

"Will you stop it?" Darius shot back. "They just want to talk, not tear me to pieces." Judging by the snarls on a couple faces, he wasn't entirely sure that was true, but he placed better odds on his safety being ensured by the rest of the protestors.

He started down the ramp. "Fine. Just please, move aside and let the men do their jobs," he called out to the leader.

It took them a few moments of milling about to settle on which side of the ramp they'd move to, and Darius had already descended and come face to face with the man who spoke for them. Noxious diesel exhaust from the passing crawler filled his nostrils, and he waved his hand near his face in a futile effort to disperse it more quickly. Darius

26   J.C. Rainier

took quick note of the faces he recognized.

Calvin and Alexis. Jake and Cora. Garza, Camp, and Quinn. Gail Conyers.

"What can I do for you?" Darius asked.

"Give us a break, Governor," Jake shouted from near the back of the crowd. He had several days' worth of dark stubble gracing his chin, and bags under his eyes. As he shifted his weight from foot to foot, Darius could see the colony-issued tee shirt stretch across his barrel chest, threatening to tear apart. "We've been working nonstop for over a month now on this project of yours."

"We need rest," Gail chimed in. She offered her hands and arms in front of her, displaying an assortment of blisters and burns. She had seen more than her fair share of time in the kitchens recently, and it showed. And smelled.

"I understand your concerns, folks. But we haven't reached our stockpile goal yet. I know you're all tired. So am I. But we have to press on."

"A day off won't hurt the cause, Governor," Jake replied.

Calvin was next. "And you could at least let us have our fruit back."

There we go. It had to come out.

Rationing had been in place since July. No one liked it. But the distribution was as fair as it could be. Darius had consulted with all of Concordia's medical professionals, and together they came up with the standards. Though lean, they were at least nutritious. On good days, Darius was able to loosen the restrictions slightly. It was never much; an extra pear here, an egg there. But everyone shared equally. Darius made it explicitly clear to his subordinates that anything else was unacceptable.

Darius shook his head firmly. "No, we can't. We have to stick with the rationing. Now's the time we can afford to give up all that we can spare, and we have to." The gathered crowd grumbled in disapproval. "I don't like it any more than you do."

"You're not the one making the sacrifices."

Darius tried to find the source of the accusation, but he couldn't tell who it was immediately. "I'm under the exact same rationing as everyone else."

"But you don't have to go out into the woods and pick berries while a reaper bear tries to eat you for breakfast."

Darius stood on his toes, looking toward the back of the crowd. He was barely able to make out the dissenter. He was a slender teenage boy, probably about seventeen. Pimples dotted his cheeks, and his sandy hair was a tangled mop.

"What's your name, son?"

"Kaden."

"Hi, Kaden," Darius continued in his most polished political voice, which still sounded quite fake to his own ears. "You're right that I'm not in either the hunting or foraging groups. But for the last month and a half I have spent every hour that I could either helping build the field irrigation, cutting fish and vegetables, or running errands for other people. I have made it my personal mission to make sure I'm up and working at the crack of dawn, and that I don't stop working until the sun goes down."

Kaden rolled his eyes and stepped back.

"So what do we do now, Governor?" Quinn asked. The man who was once Darius's superior officer now looked haggard, almost broken. The past year had not been kind or fortunate. "The irrigation hasn't done much to improve the crops, we can't plant anything more, and we have to range farther out each day for fewer returns."

"I know. But every scrap of food we can scrounge up is another scrap we have for winter. I can't stress enough how important that is."

"Can we at least get back to building the houses here on this side of the river?" Cora asked. "I mean, I've seen a few people just standing around with nothing to do now. Guys that were building those structures before."

Darius furrowed his brow. Idleness was not something the colony could afford. *No, we need them doing what they're supposed to.*

"As soon as we can spare them, we'll look into it. Please, just keep at it. I'm right there with you. This will all be over in another month or so."

He caught several looks of disappointment from his fellow citizens as they slowly dispersed, talking amongst each other in muted voices. All of them left but two: the McLaughlins. Darius waited for their inevitable approach.

"Give it to me straight, Governor," Calvin said, his voice tinged ever so slightly with apprehension. "How bad is it?"

Darius crossed his arms across his chest. "How badly do you want a pear right now?"

"Badly," Alexis replied quickly.

"Badly enough to die for it?" Their silence was response enough. "I wouldn't put a single person in Concordia through this if I didn't think it was necessary. Maybe I'm wrong. I hope to God I am."

Calvin nodded curtly. "I hope you are too."

Fractis in Posterum, Act II

"Gabi, stop it!" Charlotte bellowed as she tightened the bear hug she had thrown around Gabi.

Gabi was pressed to come up for air as the hold constricted her chest. Still she flailed and kicked, hissing venomously at Marya. The older girl was still on her backside, dabbing her fingers at the blood that dripped from her nose. Gabi landed a few kicks to Charlotte's legs, but the result was futile; Charlotte dragged her from the Palm Palace, through the town square, to the Vandemark home.

They were met at the door by Jeanette, whose countenance quickly turned sour.

"Again?" she asked. Exasperation and disappointment hung on the single word.

Charlotte nodded as she placed Gabi on the ground. Gabi crossed her arms and pouted.

"Marya?"

"She can't keep doing this. I can't keep tearing the two of them apart." Charlotte sighed. "I'm kicking Gabi out of school. She's not welcome back."

Gabi knew she was in trouble. Neither of the adults was happy with her, and every time she fought with Marya, she was punished. It was unfair, she thought, since Marya started the fights most of the time. She didn't want to be punished, and decided that bolting into the jungle and hiding for a while would be a good way to avoid Jeanette's wrath. But just as Gabi was about to run, Jeanette's arm shot out, grabbing her wrist. Gabi got as far as her arm would take her, but Jeanette's iron grip would not be swayed. Instead, Gabi tweaked her shoulder, and shot backward into her new mother's legs.

"For how long?" Jeanette asked, ignoring Gabi's attempted escape.

"Permanently. I'm sorry. Marya gets along with most of the rest of the kids, but Gabi can barely stand anyone. If she's not fighting with Marya, it's Karina. When it's not Karina, it's Caleb. When it's not Caleb, it's Aidan, and that sets off Marya all over again. I have to teach, and I can't do that if she's constantly disrupting class."

Jeanette pursed her lips and nodded. Her brow furrowed, and her voice grew quiet. "I understand. Thanks, Charlotte."

The teacher quickly left, retracing her steps. Gabi looked up at Jeanette. To her surprise, the look on Jeanette's face was not the harsh disapproving glare that she was certain would be there. Instead, Jeanette's eyebrows relaxed and her eyes closed for a brief moment. She led Gabi inside the cramped hut and sat her down in the corner. Rather than leaving her there to think about her actions, Jeanette took a seat on the packed dirt next to her. Will was lying on a bed of palms near the back of the tiny home, snoring lightly as he dozed.

Jeanette wrapped her arm around Gabi's shoulder and pulled her close. It had been a long time since anyone had held her in a comforting way. The last time that Gabi could recall was shortly after her mother died, when Kristin had cradled Gabi and sung her to sleep when she was sick. Though still comforting, Gabi couldn't help but feel that something was wrong, that the Vandemarks were forcing themselves to be nice, and that the touch wasn't genuine.

"Why do you keep doing this, Gabi?" she asked softly.

Gabi crossed her arms against her chest tightly. *She doesn't believe me. I didn't do it this time!*

"Gabi?" she repeated.

"I didn't do it! Marya was being mean!"

Will snorted loudly. Gabi watched him sit upright and rub the sleep from his eyes.

"People can be mean sometimes, sweetie. We don't fight with them just because they say something that's not nice," Jeanette said.

"Yes they do. Mama used to fight people all the time who were mean to her. Like when they kept saying she killed Haruka."

Jeanette sighed and tried to hug Gabi, who squirmed uncomfortably. "I know. But your mom was upset and sick at the time. She didn't really know what she was doing. You're not sick, and you should know better. You don't hit or fight with your friends."

"Marya's not my friend!"

"I know you don't like her, but you have to get along with her. You can't go to school if you can't get along with her. School is really important."

"I don't *want* to go to school. The kids are mean."

Will ambled across the room and took a seat on the other side of Gabi. "Don't listen to what they say, Gabs. Their words can't hurt you."

"Yes they can!" she protested. Anger and sadness bubbled up within her.

"Yeah? Like what?" he challenged.

Gabi's head snapped around, meeting his eyes. She glared as fiercely as she could, hoping that he would see just how hurt she was. But his smug grin stayed firmly planted on his lips.

"Marya said that Diego is why Mama killed herself. And that Diego isn't my brother."

That wiped the smirk off of Will's face in an instant. Instead, his jaw slacked, and he looked as shocked as Marya when Gabi had pushed her down and beaten her.

"Oh, sweetie," Jeanette said as she hugged her tight. It was a warm, smothering embrace, but Gabi didn't want it. She just wanted to be left alone.

"Stop it," she protested.

"Gabi, please. We want to help…"

"No!" she shouted. She slipped out of the hug and scurried quickly to the center of the room. Gabi stood up and turned to the two Vandemarks and snarled, "No. You took me from Mama before. You took me from Mama when she died."

"Because we care for you…"

"No! I don't like you! You always lie to me!"

"What?" Jeanette gasped. "Gabi, I'd never lie to you."

"Yeah?"

"Honest."

"Is Diego my brother?"

"Of course he is, sweetie."

"Then why doesn't he look like me or Mama?" she screamed angrily.

Will sighed and shook his head. Jeanette looked like she was about to burst into tears. She stammered, but couldn't say anything. Gabi knew deep down that she was looking for a lie to tell. Something that would convince her that everything was fine and Diego *was* her brother. Gabi knew it was all wrong, and she let out an anguished scream as she burst into tears. Jeanette tried to hug her again, but Gabi ducked and squirmed, then bolted from the hut, hurtling herself headlong into the thick undergrowth at the end of town. There was a root cave that she knew of just a few hundred feet from the hut, tucked close enough to be safe, but covered enough that the adults couldn't find her.

Gabi curled up into a ball and cried for a long time. It stung her deeply that the new mom that was supposed to care for her would lie, and that Marya, the girl she hated so fiercely, would be the one to tell the truth.

Diego's not my brother. Diego's why Mama killed herself. I hate Diego.

J.C. Rainier

Diabolus ad Ianuam

Cal watched the warm, orange glow spread through the dull coils of the burner sitting atop the sales counter. The tips of his fingers registered the temperature differential in the air as he stretched them out close. He had rubbed his hands so hard that they were nearly raw, and he could still feel hundreds of pinpricks underneath his skin from the icy air that permeated every nook and cranny of the building, from the shop floor to the apartment above.

After a minute of warming his hands, Cal curled his fingers around the frozen handle of a small metal pan, almost knocking over his lantern as he transferred it from the counter onto the burner. He then buried his hands deep inside the folds of the patchwork hide blanket wrapped around his body. The pan groaned as it suddenly became a buffer between a frozen brick of soup and the scorching burner. After a couple minutes of impatient waiting and clearing his sinuses, Cal saw the first signs of melt as the brick slowly shifted to one side of the pan.

Damn it, it's too cold to even heat up soup right.

Cal shuffled his feet, slowly making his way to the back door of the shop where a small thermometer was nailed to the door post. He had selected this spot, thinking that it would give him an idea of the average temperature between indoors and outdoors. In reality it was usually just a poor indicator of indoor temperature, muddled by drafts and cracks in the walls of the shop. Cal squinted, trying to make out the dark red line of the mercury in the poor light that filtered from the other room.

31 F

Shit.

Cal didn't want to think of how cold it was outside if it was below freezing inside the shop. He trudged back to the front of the shop to stir the soup, finding that only a couple more tablespoons had thawed out. He coughed and sniffed, then rubbed his nearly raw nose on his sleeve. Somewhere, about a kilometer away, the bulk of the residents of North Concordia were riding out the winter in the relative comfort of *Michael.* Cal was thoroughly regretting the decision that he and Alexis made to winter in their home.

Come on, it'll be romantic, he told his wife in September. *I can make room for our winter rations in the storeroom. Throw in a couple extra blankets, and it'll be like our own little winter getaway, right here in town. No bumping into everyone else when you get up to brush your teeth or change your clothes.*

Such a wonderful idea at the time, he remembered. Now it looked like one decision in a long series that might cost them their lives. Cal's fever was a hundred and two degrees the last time he had checked, but he was the one in better shape. Upstairs, Lexi rested in their bed, just a shell of her former self. The illness sapped her of her remaining strength with every hour, and Cal feared that she could succumb before long if Dr. Taylor's medicines didn't slow down the pneumonia.

He swirled the soup some more, submerging the last of the frozen bits beneath the slowly heating brown liquid. What was an unrecognizable brick a few minutes earlier now looked and smelled of rabbit, turnips, and carrots, accentuated with pungent Demeter spices. He began to salivate, and his stomach grumbled a loud and painful reminder of just how long it had been since he had last eaten. Today they could only afford to eat twice. Tomorrow was uncertain, as much depended on Dr. Taylor and her ability to convince Governor Owens to give up another special allotment of rations.

Ten minutes and four painful coughing fits later, the soup was close to scalding hot. Cal took the pan by the handle, using the fur blanket as a makeshift mitt to keep from scorching his hand. After he turned off the burner and grabbed the lantern, he turned up the steep stairs with his awkward load.

The tiny second floor apartment was only a few degrees warmer. Though what little heat that was present inside rose to the second floor, the inefficient slats of the wooden window shutter easily allowed any vital warmth to escape. There was always a draft, flowing from the rear door of the shop, up the stairs, and out the window. During the summer this had been a modest blessing. The biting winter chill made it a terrible curse. The blanket he had secured over the window only mitigated the problem slightly. A small fire crackled weakly in the stone fireplace, but most of the heat it produced was sucked straight up the chimney. If he had an effective way to do so, Cal would have blocked it off as well.

Cal set the lantern down on their dresser, a waist-high affair cobbled together with remnants from the lumber mill. Three species of wood used in its construction gave it an odd mosaic-like appearance. It had no drawers; instead, there were sectioned off shelves where wicker baskets could easily be slid out from the front. Their only other piece of furniture was a mattress, which rested on the floor against the wall next to the dresser. It wasn't until Cal was in a world without heating and air conditioning that he finally understood the purpose of bed-frames and box springs.

Alexis was curled up in a tight ball underneath the covers. A thick blanket of brown fur covered the bed completely. It was tucked under the mattress at its foot, and each side draped onto the floor and wadded up from its sheer size. This was the warmest blanket they owned, cut and sewn from the hide of a reaper bear, the deadliest predator on the planet. On the floor next to Alexis rested another pot, the handle of a wooden spoon jutting out from inside. Cal tugged at the thinner blanket that draped over him, loosening it at the knees so he could kneel comfortably next to his wife.

He stroked her sweaty forehead. She startled awake, her sunken green eyes darting around in confusion, her gaunt cheeks puffing out like balloons as she coughed. Cal knew that the heavy bear pelt disguised even more of her illness's disturbing effects. She had lost a lot of weight. Without a scale he couldn't say how much, but Alexis no longer had her beautiful, captivating curves. When she undressed he could see her ribs and hips protruding sickly under her skin. Her skin, though pale before, was now ashen.

Damn it, Doc. How much longer before she gets better?

"Dinner time," he smiled, suppressing any signs of worry.

Alexis moaned weakly and closed her eyes. "Too tired. Too early. Let me sleep."

"No, hon. You've been sleeping all day. You need to eat something."

"Or else what?" Though soft, her voice carried a sharply irritated tone.

"Or you don't get better," he snapped back.

"A little sleep isn't going to kill me."

"It might. God damn it, Lexi, you need to listen to me."

"I need to sleep," she mumbled, curling deeper into the blanket

Cal set the soup pan on the floor, then leaned over to hug and caress her. "You need to get better."

She neither responded nor opened her eyes. By the way her chest rose and fell as she breathed she must have fallen asleep again.

C'mon, Lexi. I need you to pull through. You can't leave me here alone.

* * *

Jacob Granger
18 Jan, 2 yal, 14:56
>|

Any minute now, he thought. *Any minute he'll come downstairs and make dinner.*

His fingers trembled terribly. If anyone had asked, Jake would have told them it was just the cold. But he knew better. His nerves had his fingers twitching and his stomach tied in a tight knot. It was just below freezing outside, yet his palms sweated. The cold steel tucked into his waistband felt even icier than the wind cutting through the dark night. Not because it was physically cold. He knew better. He knew it represented desperation and death.

Jake cupped his hands to his bearded face, blowing into them and rubbing them together to stave off the cold, though the warmth of his exhaust could do nothing to alleviate the tremors of guilt. He glanced up at the second story window of the small shop along the river. Soft yellow light filtered through the shutter's slats. He saw what he thought was movement. His breathing stopped. Seconds passed. Daggers of pain shot through the exposed tips of his fingers, but he didn't break his focus.

After a few more moments the light from the shutters dimmed and faded. Jake exhaled loudly and closed his eyes. To the forefront of his mind came images of his wife and children. Cora's bright smile and curly locks cut through the darkness as she snuggled their three month old son. Gregarious little Alex bounded up, throwing his arms around his mother and then kissing his brother's forehead.

Jake opened his eyes. The soft light now pulsed and throbbed from the lower level window at the front of the shop. He exhaled again and put one foot in front of the other, crunching through the thin layer of ice atop the six inches of snow. Ice turned to slush in his boots, drenching his socks and chilling his nearly numb toes, but he continued on. His heart beat furiously inside his chest with every step he took. Nearly every fiber of his being screamed at him to turn back, that it wasn't too late.

But in his mind and his heart, it was too late. Cora was slowly wasting away. While still healthy, she worried about baby Earl. Alex constantly complained of the pain gnawing at his stomach. Jake felt it too; the constant emptiness of hunger. But for a four-year-old boy fueled by growth spurts, it was unimaginable. Nor did Jake want to imagine it, let alone have his son suffer from it.

Jake reached the front door of the shop. He rapped on the roughly planked door with his left hand. His right reached to his waistband and switched off the Beretta's safety. Jake drew in a deep breath and waited.

Nothing happened. He wasn't sure why, but he started counting under his breath. Ten seconds. Fifteen. Thirty. He knocked again, unsure if he was heard the first time. Ten seconds. Fifteen.

Just before he reached thirty, he heard the knob on the door turn. The door cracked open. He hesitated for a second, his conscience bargaining with him at the last second.

"Jake?" Cal asked.

Jake snapped back to reality. He slammed his right boot into the door jamb and drew the pistol, aiming it from his hip. Cal's eyes widened and he tried to slam the door on Jake's frozen boot. The heavy door sent stabbing pains through Jake's foot. He bit his lip to stifle a yelp of pain, but pushed into the door as hard as he could with his left shoulder. He was much larger than Cal, and the younger man stumbled and fell backward. A patchwork fur blanked that he had been wearing crumpled to the floor haphazardly. Jake retrained the weapon on his neighbor.

"Where is it?" he asked, his voice hoarse from laryngitis.

"J-Jake, don't do this," Cal pleaded, backpedaling desperately on his rear.

"I don't want to hurt you, man. Just… just give it to me. That's all I want."

Cal scrambled his way to the sales counter, where he was able to regain his feet. On top sat a lantern and a portable electric burner. Atop the burner was a metal pot, and as Jake predicted, something was cooking. He was hit by the smells of spiced broth and vegetables. He instantly recognized the soup made from native root vegetables. It was something he had the pleasure of smelling nearly every day for much of the summer and fall. Cora was assigned to the team of colonists responsible for canning and preserving the harvest, and the soup was her specialty. So much of her time and effort had gone into creating these rations for the colony, and now Cal was cooking a serving of it. A serving he hadn't earned.

"Jake, stop it. Please. Just… just go away and I won't tell Darius about it."

"Darius?" he spat. "I know you've been getting more rations than the rest of us. I've seen Doc and Hunter bringing them to you. You've got only two mouths to feed. Darius probably wants to know that you've been stealing food."

Cal's eyes widened. "Stealing? You think I've been…"

"Yes, stealing." The sweat on Jake's palms was making his grip on the pistol somewhat tenuous, so he readjusted as subtly as he could. Though Calvin was stealing from the colony, what Jake was doing was no better. Only necessary.

"I'm not stealing. I swear."

Jake took two steps forward. He changed his aim from Cal's stomach to his head. "Show me where it is," he commanded sternly.

Cal's hands trembled as he raised them into the air. He looked as if he was about to wet himself, but somehow he managed to stay composed enough to speak.

"This way. In my stock room."

Cal walked slowly ahead of Jake, who grabbed the lantern off the counter with his free hand. As they passed the stairwell a weak female voice called down to them.

"Cal, honey? Is everything okay?"

Without prompting, he replied, "Yeah, everything's fine. I'll be up in a minute."

Jack was taken aback. He expected Cal to shout out a warning about Jake, and yell to her to jump out the window and find help. Instead, the twenty-year-old man continued on, slowly reaching for the stock room door and opening it. Jake slipped by, keeping his weapon trained nervously on his neighbor. Cal just looked at the floor and folded his arms across his chest.

Jake quickly took stock of what he could see on the sparsely stocked shelves. Most of what remained was soap from Cal's business. A mostly empty barrel of pickled fish sat near the door. A couple dozen jars of soup, a couple bags of jerky, three bags of crackers, and two bags of black eyed peas were all that was left. Jake's heart sank. The treasure trove of food that he had imagined didn't actually exist.

"You ate it all," he sighed.

"Only the extras that Doctor Taylor prescribed."

"Prescribed?" Jake almost choked on the word.

"Check the wooden box to your right. Third shelf down."

Jake scanned the shelf and found a small box that he had originally dismissed. He pointed to it, and Cal nodded solemnly. Jake opened the top to reveal three pill bottles. He picked one up and read the label.

He didn't know exactly what the medicine was, but knew enough to recognize that it was a prescription from Dr. Taylor.

"Which one of you is sick?" he asked. Every word seemed a bitterer pill than the one before.

"Both of us. The meds are for Lexi."

Jake swallowed. The lump in his throat tightened even more. "With what?"

Cal shrugged and motioned back to the front of the shop, then turned away. Jake took a moment's pause, biting his lip and bowing his head, before catching up. "Nasty cold at first," Cal said. "Lexi's got pneumonia now. That's why Doc's been getting us extra rations. She might die otherwise."

Jake watched his neighbor swirl the pan to stir the soup. The tantalizing smell was driving him to salivate, and his hunger returned with a vengeance. The urge to kill his neighbor and feast on the meager meal was gaining momentum. Then Jake remembered his own family, huddled somewhere in the dark and cold recesses of an apartment just a few hundred feet away.

Just get what you came for, he thought.

Cal had wrapped the blanket around himself again, and was holding the soup pan in his left hand, blanket as a barrier from the heat. He looked expectantly, if not pleadingly, at Jake. The plan was unraveling. He couldn't make up his mind between murder and surrender.

"Please. Lexi needs to eat."

"So do we," he blurted.

Cal nodded solemnly. "I know. I really know what you're going through. Please, just put the gun away and come upstairs with me."

Jake lowered the barrel just an inch or two, hesitating as he processed Cal's request.

"I'm not going to try anything," Cal continued. "Please, just don't freak Lexi out."

Jake sighed and lowered the weapon, turning on the safety before tucking it away. Cal nodded and walked up the stairs, beckoning for Jake to follow. He did so, and when they reached the top, he nearly dropped to his knees in horror.

The McLaughlins were very prominent in Concordia. Cal's reputation, earned during Unification, had put him in high regard with many. He had his own business making soap and biodiesel for the colony. Cal was also known as a prolific barterer, trading his own service shrewd-ly for that of others. Many in the colony, Jake included, believed that they had almost instantly become a wealthy and prosperous family. It was why Jake targeted them as soon as he found out they were stealing food. Or so it had seemed.

Reality set in quickly for Jake. The McLaughlins were, at best, liv-ing on par with everyone else in the colony. They had next to nothing in their apartment. A single dresser. A bed. A couple nice blankets. A pantry that wouldn't last the winter. And an extremely ill spouse.

Cal knelt next to his wife, who was staring at Jake through sullen eyes. "Hey, Lex. Jake came to see us. He wanted to see how you're do-ing."

Jake put on a fake smile, prompted by Cal's outright lie. "Hi Alexis. Sorry to hear you're under the weather," he said as he timidly took a few steps forward. He kept his hands firmly in his pocket, crossing his front. He didn't want to chance her seeing the gun.

She smiled weakly. "Hey, Jake. How's Cora? I miss her so much."

Her sweet, innocent words drove a lance through his heart. There was no way that this woman, who was all skin and bones, bedridden and coughing, could have been stealing maliciously from the commu-nity. She just needed food and medicine. And through it all, she still thought of Cora.

"She's fine," he choked back his emotion, barely able to maintain his façade. "She's in love with another guy though. I'm pretty sure Earl's stolen her heart. But what can you do, right? Little stinker's got such pinchable cheeks."

"Aww, that's cute," she fawned. "Give them my love."

Cal took his wife's hands in his. "I've got to go talk to Jake for a minute. You eat up, okay? I'll be up in a minute for bed."

Jake went back downstairs, unable to watch the display of affec-tion any longer. He was wrong about the McLaughlins, and it was tearing him up inside. At the same time, his own family needed food. Even though what was left in Cal's store room wasn't enough for the McLaughlins to survive the winter, the Granger family had even less. And more mouths to feed. He stumbled into the front of the shop and collapsed, his back to the counter, his head buried in his hands. He couldn't win. If he robbed his neighbor, his family would eat for a little longer, but Alexis might die. If he went home, it would be empty hand-ed, to three more starving mouths. Jake broke down and cried, unable to handle the pressure any longer.

Minutes passed. It could have been nearly an hour, for all Jake knew. He struggled endlessly with the moral quandary. But his neighbor ended it for him. Jake felt something nudge his foot. He looked down through bleary eyes to see a wooden crate. Inside were a bag of crackers, a bag of jerky, a bag of beans, and two jars of soup.

"W-what?" he gasped, looking up at the tall, lanky young man.

"Go. Take this."

Jake clamored to his feet. He wiped his eyes and snorted, clearing his nose. "N-no. I… I can't."

"It's what you came here for."

"No, Alexis needs this."

Cal shook his head and nudged the crate with his foot. "This isn't hers. This is mine."

Jake's heart dropped. He understood the sacrifice that Cal was offering. "No. You'll starve to death."

"Better me than your boys."

Jake rose to his feet and met Cal's eyes. He shook his head vehemently. "No. No, I can't."

"You will. Or I'll tell Darius what happened." Cal's eyes were stern and his gaze was grim. "Take this and leave. That's your only option."

Jake had little doubt that he'd be true to his word. He bent down and collected the hefty crate. Jake nodded at his neighbor, and without a word exited through the front door, which was held open for him.

Four hundred feet away, in front of the door to his apartment, Jake's knees gave out as adrenaline wore off and guilt overcame him.

J.C. Rainier

Cal, wake up.

Alexis. Her voice was so far away. It echoed as if coming from beyond a faraway hill, yet it was closer than that. He licked his lips and turned over.

Cal, God damn it, wake up!

In a minute, he responded.

It was so very hot. Balmy, actually. Bravo's sun beat down on his brow from high above, filtered by thousands of tiny mesquite leaves.

"There's no mesquite, idiot," his own voice lectured.

"Huh?"

"Demeter. There's no mesquite on Demeter, stupid."

Cal was truly beginning to despise his alternate self. He was trying to remember how long it had been since he came back. Four days? Five? Keeping track had become a chore, and not one that Cal particularly relished.

"Sure there are. Over at the... uhm..."

"Texas," the doppelganger replied dryly.

"Yeah, over at the Texas."

Cal? C'mon, Cal.

"Wow. You really are brain dead, aren't you?"

"Shut up."

"Make me."

"Sure. Just give me a chance to talk to Doc," Cal grinned.

I'm here, Calvin. What do you want to talk about? Distinctly Dr. Taylor, yet distinctly far away.

"Oh, you're talking to her alright."

Cal sat up, shielding his eyes from the bright sun to get a better look at his spectral tormentor. "What the hell are you talking about?"

His double cupped his hands over his mouth and raised his voice to a shout. "You're dying, stupid."

Cal lay back down in the grass. "No tunnel, no angels, no lights."

"OK, so what's that big ball of fusion up there?"

"The sun."

"Think that might be a light?"

Cal ignored his double.

"Do I have to sing for you? I mean, I'm not a fat lady, but I'm pretty sure it's about the same in the end."

"Oh, I'm sure your voice is so lovel.. AARGH!"

Cal's though was cut short by an intense stabbing pain that ran through his arm. He bolted upright, clawing at the site of the pain. There was a tiny but bright red spot on his skin that wasn't there a moment before.

"Got your attention yet?"

"What the fuck was that?"

I'm sorry, Calvin. Dr. Taylor again.

"A needle."

"Huh?"

Alexis and Dr. Taylor were talking. He couldn't understand them. They were so far away. Someone else was there too. Someone familiar, but Cal couldn't figure out who. He was dreaming again, another unsettling dream, like those during hibernation aboard *Michael*.

His doppelganger closed its eyes and its arms rose from its side, as if he was feeling the sun on his face after a long winter's slumber.

"Do you feel it coming?" it asked. A haunting, chilling question in alien context.

"What the hell is going on?"

Damn it, he's seizing. Dr. Taylor again.

"You're really going to make me repeat myself?"

"I'm dying," Cal gasped.

His twin nodded. "On the bright side, it's a noble death. Jake will tell everyone how you sacrificed yourself to save his family." A cruel, twisted grin spread across his mirrored face. "Oh wait, he won't. Because if the truth came out, he would be torn from his family, and Darius would put him in stasis."

Cal swallowed hard, even as his fingers and toes grew numb. "It doesn't matter. I know the truth. Alexis will think it was for her."

"Or that you're an idiot who couldn't count. Either case, it's been nice knowing you." There was an awkward pause. "Oh come on, that was a good one. Laugh a little."

Cal lay back on the grass once more, looking up at the Texas sky for one last time.

She couldn't control her tears. Not that she wanted to. The love of her life, the man who saved her from death, the man who was the very reason she breathed, lay on their bed upstairs. Cal had been at her side the whole time, tending to her every need, even as he had fallen ill himself. His fever was rampant, and the seizures were growing worse. Alexis wanted to be with him through it all, but Darius had pulled her away.

Doctor Taylor needs to concentrate, he had insisted. He had carried her down the stairs like Cal would have carried a sack of grain. Her sapped strength from her own ordeal prevented her from fighting back. *Let Doc do her job.*

No, I want to be with him. If… if he goes, I need… she had protested.

It won't come to that. I promise.

It was the promise that swayed her. Not her weakness and inability to help. Not her burning desire to be with her gravely ill husband. It was the calm, solemn, and sincere promise of the Hero of Concordia. The promise that if she let Dr. Taylor work uninterrupted, Cal would survive.

But that was almost an hour ago. Guilt and fear were her enemies just as much as the clock. She hadn't heard anything in an hour, and it was killing her inside. Mercy had to come at some point. Mercy in the form of news. Mercy in grief or relief. Alexis was growing too tired to care which it was.

Then the footsteps came. Alexis took two deep breaths to stem the tears. She craned her neck to hear, anxious to know whether they were the doctor's light steps, or the governor's solid stride. As she choked on her tears, she realized it was both. They emerged at nearly the same time. Worry was written on both of their faces.

"Doctor?" she sobbed.

"He's stable," she said, wringing her wrinkled hands. "At least for now. He can't stay here. He'll die of exposure before his body can even think of fighting off the infection."

Alexis's lips trembled and she buried her head in her hands. "Oh God. Oh God, please don't let him die."

"He won't," Darius assured. "I made a promise to you, and I'll be damned if I don't keep it."

"We're going to move him to *Michael* as soon as we can," the doctor added. "There's heat there, and I can keep a closer eye on him, too."

Alexis flew off of her perch on the counter and threw her tiny arms around Dr. Taylor's neck. "Oh my God, *thank you.*"

The doctor returned a light embrace, but then gently pushed Alexis out to arm's length, keeping a firm grasp on her shoulders and looking into her eyes. The concern was no less apparent than when she came down from the loft. "He's not out of the woods yet. The fever is burning up his brain. Even if he survives, I can't guarantee he'll be the same afterwards."

Alexis could only contain her fear and anxiety for a few moments. As bravely as she met the news, she could only manage to keep her emotions in check so far. She sobbed softly as the doctor and the governor left the shop.

"I'm sorry, Alexis. We'll do what we can," Governor Owens said as he cinched the belt on his heavy overcoat and stepped through the portal into the heavy, slushy snow.

Vocatum Messorem

Chief James Vandemark
12 April, 2 yal, early morning
Camp Eight
>|

As he parted the storm curtain, a wall of grotesque air knocked him back and turned his stomach sour in an instant. James gagged and coughed, trying to clear the stench of stewing vomit from his sinuses. Once he was certain that he wouldn't throw up, James secured a make-shift handkerchief, cut from a torn flight suit, over his nose and mouth.

The doctor wasn't kidding, he thought.

James entered the clinic. His eyes took a moment to adjust to the darkness, and the rag did little to reduce the stench. He had to force back the urge to vomit, a task made more difficult with every step he took. All eight beds in the clinic were occupied. Other patients filled the gaps between the beds, lying on the dirt or propped up against the wall. Moans of discomfort were accentuated every few seconds by someone retching. Shivers ran down James's spine as he took in the pitiful scene. Dr. Petrovsky rested against the short partition wall near the rear, doubled over in agony. It was he who was the source of the retching noises.

Shit.

Emilia emerged from behind the partition with a folded cloth, which she held against the doctor's brow until his spasms stopped and he could take it from her. She scurried up to meet James, worry clearly evident on her normally stony face.

"How is he?" James asked.

"Well, I wouldn't want to be him, that's for sure." She sighed and shook her head. "He's in the early stages. It's only going to get worse for him."

James nodded. The disease borne by the survivors of the Lake Raphael settlement had never really gone away. The sick were quarantined until they recovered. The village would go a few weeks without any incident, and then a new case would crop up. At first they were only from the haggard group of refugees led by Daniels, but eventually Camp Eight's residents had fallen ill. Until a week ago, it was never more than one or two cases at a time.

That was when the disease flared up with a cluster of eight new cases. In that short span, almost fifty residents of Camp Eight had either become ill, or started to experience symptoms. Doctor Petrovsky took as many as he could into the clinic, the rest were waiting at the Palm

Palace. James grimaced as he took another look at the stricken doctor, who looked pale and emaciated, even from twenty feet away. The medical staff was now down to just two: Emilia and Patricia.

One for each building. Damn.

"Any idea on how to fight it?" he asked.

"No. Hell, the other group never figured it out. All they did was drag it here with them."

"Nothing at all?" The news was unsettling, and it made him clutch his makeshift mask tighter against his face.

"No. Shit, Chief, I don't even know if we're dealing with something bacterial, viral, or fungal. And if this thing is a prion, we've got no chance in hell. Might as well lock us all in the Palace and set it on fire."

James swallowed hard. "Is it fatal?"

"Probably. No one who's caught it since those refugees arrived has died, but if what I've heard from some of those people is true, it's a killer. Horrible death, too. You don't want to know about it."

"Maybe not, but I need to know. It's my responsibility."

Emilia nodded and cast a quick sideways glance at one of the patients. "High fever. Vomiting and extreme diarrhea. Slow recovery time. A great cocktail for dying from any number of issues, not the least of which are starvation and dehydration. I hate to say it, but I think the fever would be the best way to go, because at some point you'd either go into a coma, or your brain would be so cooked that you wouldn't be able to comprehend what's happening."

James scowled harshly at the nurse. "You mean you'd rather someone die as a vegetable?"

"Would you rather die of thirst because you can't keep it down?" she shot back. "Because I've heard from the other colonists that's what happened to a lot of people."

James shuddered. The sounds of suffering came at him from every angle, and he couldn't bear to be in the clinic any more. "Just keep me updated," he said tersely as he left.

He stormed down the path toward the sea. As soon as the clinic was out of sight he tore the mask from his face and drew in deep breaths of the salty air. It wasn't until he reached the beach that he could no longer smell remnants of the vile disease. James tried to convince himself that this was all a trick of the mind, and that whatever force responsible for the disease was contained as best as it could be. But he couldn't help noticing that the beach was nearly deserted at a time of day that should have been prime for fishermen and young children.

I need to talk to Daniels and find out just what the hell she knows.

Karen grunted and strained as she tried in vain to keep the logs from falling out of position as she wrapped the thick cord of vines around them. Her knees ached from kneeling on the hard, uneven wood for too long, and her hands were raw and blistered. She was close to finishing her project, but for every step she completed in the canoe's construction, mounting fatigue slowed her progress.

Damn it. This should be done already.

"Can you give me a hand with this?" she asked Mina.

The younger woman turned away from her work collecting salt from the trunk of a mighty palm tree. Her strides were impossibly long for a woman of her height, Karen thought as Mina covered the distance in only four steps.

"What do you need me to do?"

"I'm going to hold these two logs together. I need you to lash them to the pylon there."

Mina nodded and knelt in the dirt in front of the pylon, straddling the logs that would make up the crude outrigger. She slipped the rope into position and nodded to Karen. Karen squeezed the timbers together with all her might, then lifted slightly upward to allow Mina to double up the rope if needed. Mina's hands worked quickly, wrapping and weaving the two logs together.

"Up a little more," she said.

Karen sucked in a deep breath and pulled her arms closer to her chest. She could feel the logs wobble slightly as her arms trembled in exhaustion.

"Hurry up," she panted.

"Just a moment."

Karen gritted her teeth. Rivulets of sweat rolled from her brow. Just as her strength was about to fail, she felt the weight slack. Karen glanced over her shoulder to find that Chief Vandemark had come to her aid. A minute later Mina finished lashing the logs to the pylon, and the completed canoe was gently lowered back to the ground.

"Thanks," Karen puffed.

"Not a problem," James replied.

"How's Jack?" Mina asked as she took a seat on the edge of the craft.

"Worse than yesterday, I'm afraid."

Karen grimaced. The symptoms all fit. It looked as if the mysterious jungle disease had come back. Survivors of all stripes were being affected, even those who had previously fought off the illness. She was not surprised, but definitely concerned for what this might mean. James crossed his arms across his slender frame and leaned against a short vinewood. She could feel his stare piercing her, judging her.

"You knew this would happen, didn't you?" he said. His voice was low and soft, but there was no mistaking his disapproval and anger.

"We didn't know."

"Don't jerk me around, Daniels."

"We didn't know it would happen," she insisted. Her muscles tensed as she rebuked the accusation. "Everything we knew about the disease suggested that the salt air next to the coast would stop it."

"And the sick people you traveled with? Some of them died. That should have been a clue," he growled.

"They were all infected before we left Lake Raphael! We buried our dead along the way. Everyone who survived was able to make it and recovered in your quarantine camp. No one new got sick."

"Until after you got here."

Karen sighed. There was no way to deny that. There was no rampant disease in Camp Eight before their arrival. And what tore through the populace was too similar to be a coincidence. "Until we got here," she admitted.

"You've brought a world of shit to my doorstep, Daniels." His tone returned to that of cold anger.

"I'm sorry. We really thought this wouldn't happen."

"Because of what your medical staff told you."

"Yes."

"The staff that died from this. Every single one."

"Hey! Brett tried to find a cure," Mina protested.

"I wasn't talking to you, little girl," he snapped.

"Hey," Daniels barked, taking two long, furious strides toward the chief. "You don't talk to her that way."

James straightened up and looked Karen in the eyes. Even though he exuded an air of confidence, she couldn't help but notice that he was two inches shorter than she. Despite that, he was an intimidating force. Perhaps it was his position of power, or perhaps he was just crazy enough to go toe to toe with her anyway.

"You don't talk to her that way," she repeated firmly.

"She doesn't speak unless spoken to," he hissed. "Or so help me I will throw her out of this village."

"You wouldn't dare."

"Try me. You'll be next." His brown eyes burned with an intensity she hadn't seen in years. "You've got no chips left, Daniels. Your people are sick, out of food, and far from home. If you want them to stay in this village, you do exactly what I say. You answer any damn question I ask. And your lieutenants do not question or interrupt me. Ever. Do I make myself clear?"

Karen clenched her teeth and nodded. She felt sick to her stomach that she had to comply with this diminutive dictator, but she had no choice. He was right; she had no cards left to play. Her people were entirely at his mercy, and mercy hinged on utter compliance.

"Crystal," she grumbled.

"Good. Now tell me why this Brett guy thought that the disease would go away if you moved to the coast."

Karen sighed, calling back to mind the dozens of conversations she had with Brett Wu before the plague took him. "We had sent scouts in all directions to try to find anything that might fight the sickness. Two of the teams never got sick. At least, not when they were scouting. The only thing we could figure out was that they were the ones scouring the coast to the south. Otherwise they were the same as any other team."

"Can I talk to them?"

"No. Three of them fell sick and died after they were pulled from scouting duty. The last one was killed by a jaguar."

"Unfortunate," James remarked dryly. Karen balled her fist, her patience with his callousness wearing thing. "So why are survivors getting sick again?"

"I don't know. I'm not a doctor."

"Did Brett have any ideas?"

How could he have?

She shook her head. "He was the first to fall ill for a second time."

"I see. Do you have anyone left who hasn't fallen sick a second time?"

Karen exchanged glances with Mina, who nodded. "Mina hasn't. I haven't. There are probably a dozen or so more."

"Understood." His voice warmed only slightly. "I want a list. Once Doctor Petrovsky recovers I want you two to work with him on figuring this out. I want to know if there's a reason why some of you have only been sick once. It might be our best shot at stopping whatever this is."

If Doctor Petrovsky recovers, you mean. She nodded in agreement. Chief Vandemark left the two women without a word of apology or gratitude.

"What an asshole," Mina blurted.

Karen shook her head and turned her attention back to the canoe, inspecting the integrity of the new outrigger. "Don't let him hear you say that. We can't afford to piss him off again."

Mina caught her by the arm and turned Karen to face her. The younger woman made no effort to hide her disgust and indignity. "You're just going to take that from him?"

"Yes," she replied without skipping a beat. "And so will you. For Jack's sake. For everyone's sake."

Karen Daniels
19 April, 2 yal, mid morning
>|

A distant crack echoed through the air, barely audible over the calls of the gulls that circled above. Karen barely noticed; it was mating season for many species of animals, and jaguars were particularly aggressive this time of year. But jaguars didn't swim in the open ocean, and the catch that filled the canoe's miniscule hold was in no danger.

Denise broke through the surface of the water like a missile. The torrent of sea water that ran down sprayed forth as it met her lips, cast away as she purged the spent air from her lungs. Karen turned her head slightly to the right instinctively. She then felt the canoe dip slightly to the left as Denise grabbed hold of the outrigger. Karen turned back toward her partner with an outstretched hand and retrieved a course, woven net that was offered to her. She dumped its contents into the basket at her feet. Large crustaceans and mollusks spilled forth, crawling over each other in an effort to skitter to safety. Karen quickly turned the net inside out and secured it over the basket's maw, sealing the creatures' escape path.

The canoe listed further as Denise climbed over the gunnels and took her seat at the bow. Karen took a moment to study her partner's mood. Denise had insisted that she was coping fine before they shoved off at dawn. But she had barely spoken more than two words all day, and taken to Karen's commands without question or attitude.

She's not handling this well, Karen thought, chewing on her lip. *She hasn't talked back. Not once.*

Karen realized that she was staring, and that Denise glared back at her with a furrowed brow.

"What?" Denise snapped.

"It's Jack, isn't it?"

Denise shook her head and rolled her eyes, then turned away. She drew her oar from the hull with a deliberate motion and sunk it deep into the crystal water. Karen silently paddled on the same side until the canoe was pointed at the shore, then alternated to keep the course steady. Another distant gunshot echoed through the silence.

It's Jack, she confirmed silently.

Though the canoe was barely fifteen feet long and full of fish, the distance between Karen and Denise felt more like a growing chasm. Denise still held her partially to blame for her first husband's death.

Karen couldn't blame her either, even though it was all circumstantial. Lieutenant Cormack had to move the survivors from their landing site because there was no drinkable water. And there was no way to know about the jungle disease, or if staying put was any less of a death sentence. Denise nearly died when the band had finally reached Lake Raphael. Her husband wasn't so lucky.

Now her second husband, Jack, was on death's door. The plague ravaged him for the second time, and his body was reduced to a withered husk. Jack's hopes of survival were slim at best; the village's entire medical staff was now out of commission, and the few volunteers who dared to approach the sick were ill trained to handle such an outbreak. Karen feared that she might lose her most trusted lieutenant, and the thought sickened her. But whatever thoughts were eating at Denise must have been unfathomably dark.

They paddled ashore in silence. Karen dragged the craft as far out of the water as far as she could, then followed Denise's lead in unloading the morning's catch. Two more shots rang out in rapid succession. Karen set down her baskets and looked at the nearly bald hill where the village square sat.

"Must be a lot of jaguars today," she said in hopes to spark a conversation. Denise didn't react to the attempt at small talk.

What finally garnered a reaction from the brooding woman was something that caught Karen's attention as well. Three more gunshots rang out from the hill, followed a few seconds later by an eruption of weapons fire. Two distinct varieties of shots could be heard; the deeper, louder reports of rifle rounds overwhelmed the sound from the smaller pistols. She dropped her basket and sprinted toward the rear of pod eleven's wreck, where she had left her belt and holster. As Karen retrieved the belt and strapped it hurriedly around her waist, Denise bolted past, shrieking Jack's name over and over hysterically.

There's no way that's wildlife.

Karen broke into a sprint, chasing Denise up the hill. A large plume of white-gray smoke began to rise from the town's center. As they approached the base she could hear screaming. Panicked villagers rushed headlong down the hill, even as the sound of gunfire died out. Karen slowed just enough to draw her weapon and disengage the safety before picking up speed again. A woman and two children cried out in alarm as soon as they saw Karen, diving from the side of the path into a thick, thorny bush.

What the hell?

As Karen charged up the path, everyone she encountered had a similar reaction. An eerie feeling wrapped around her, and she suddenly found it difficult to breathe. She was nearly to the village when another barrage was unleashed. Karen could hear rounds hit the dirt and the trees just above her head, and she instinctively dropped to the ground and rolled toward cover. Her heart raced as Denise disappeared into the village. Another shot hit a tree close to her, and the spent slug slammed into the ground about an inch from her arm.

Fuck, she thought as she drew her arm in as tightly as she could. Karen knew that Denise was running right in to trouble, but fear rooted Karen to the ground. Any chance she had to run the other woman down and find cover for both of them passed with the hesitation.

Moments later, Denise's shrill voice pierced the air, shouting obscenities. Someone else shouted a command in return. A male, though it was hard for her to tell who over the chaos. Then two shots rang out. More screams and chaos. Karen could see Mina hunkered down behind the wall of one of the huts on the town's edge. She peeked out from behind her cover to look into the village square ever so briefly before pulling back. That's when she caught Mina's eyes. Even the distance could not conceal Mina's fear; her eyes were like full moons, and the barrel of the pistol she clutched trembled under her death grip.

The jungle canopy rustled loudly, heralding a change in the wind. Smoke poured out from between the buildings. Karen lost sight of Mina for a few seconds, but picked her up again a few minutes, running through the smoke. Five loud reports from a rifle, and Mina's chest and legs twisted and jerked. She tumbled forward, losing her grip on her weapon as soon as she hit the dirt.

"NO!" Karen screamed.

Mina skidded to a stop in a jumbled, bloodied heap just a few feet from Karen. With only a second's hesitation Karen lunged for her lieutenant, grabbed her by the arms, and dragged her to cover. She was still alive, though Karen knew she didn't have much time to get help. Mina had been shot in the right hip twice and once each in the left arm and chest, just under her right breast. The blood that oozed from the chest wound bubbled as air escaped the punctured lung. Karen dropped her pistol at her side, freeing her hands to put pressure on the wound. It did absolutely nothing to stop the bleeding.

"Shit," she cursed under her breath. Karen looked around desperately for anyone else, but the trail was now completely abandoned. "Medic," she bellowed. "I need a medic!"

"No," Mina gurgled.

"Shh," Karen hissed. "Don't talk."

"Rr..rr… run."

"What?" She shook her head. "No, I'm not leaving you. Someone will get us help." Karen raised her voice again. "Medic!"

Mina brought her hand up and weakly pushed Karen's shoulder. "Rr..un." What was left of her voice was fading fast, and blood sprayed Karen's face when she coughed.

Something inside Karen told her to obey Mina. She could hear angry shouts getting closer, but the swirling smoke obscured her view of the village. She could only make out the outline of the closest hut. Mina hissed something else, but there wasn't clarity to understand. Karen retrieved her weapon and stood to flee. As soon as she did so, she heard Seth's booming voice from nearby.

"Drop it!" he bellowed.

The command came from a dark silhouette, partially hidden by the wall of the hut. There was also the familiar, unmistakable outline of a carbine, just barely visible through the smoke. She did as he demanded. Her weapon fell to the dirt with a thud.

"N..no," Mina croaked, which triggered another coughing fit.

Karen raised her hands in surrender. She glanced down just long enough to watch Mina expire. Whether she drowned in her own blood or suffocated thanks to the hole in her chest didn't matter. Either was horrific. When Karen dared to look up again, Seth was just a few feet away, his M4 pointed directly in her face. Someone else had taken his position behind the hut, covering Seth in case she tried anything stupid.

Seth prodded Mina's lifeless body with his toe, then stepped over it to move behind Karen. "Go," he commanded sternly.

He didn't say where to go, but then again he didn't need to. The village was the only logical place, even though something terrible had happened. She had no idea just how terrible until she was walking through it.

The first body she encountered was Denise's. She was sprawled face down in the dirt, a pool of blood radiating from her chest. Her dead gaze was fixed somewhere in the expanse of the jungle. From there on was a steadily increasing field of bodies that lead to the heart of the village. Men, women and children rested where they were cut down. Some in each others' arms, others alone. It didn't matter where they came from, either. Karen recognized friends from Lake Raphael lying next to original Camp Eight settlers. Some were armed, and died fighting where they stood, while others were shot in the back as they fled. Smoke and flames billowed from two huts near the center of the settlement.

It was too much for Karen to comprehend. Her feet grew heavier with every corpse she passed. There were dozens, perhaps even a hundred. She quickly stopped counting for fear that putting a number to it all would make her lose control, and that she'd try to fight Seth. He shadowed silently behind her. For an ephemeral moment the idea made sense, and she tried to calculate the odds of at least taking him down before his companion could finish her. But there would be no point, except to make two more bodies to bury.

She was ushered into a hut with thirteen others. Neither Seth nor his escort ventured inside; it was apparent that this was to be her prison for now. Karen slumped against a wall to give her brain a chance to catch up with the carnage from outside. But again that process was put on hold as she quickly realized that everyone around her was from Lake Raphael. These were all her people, and every one of them was wounded.

The Morgan brothers had both been shot. Trevor's skin was ghostly pale, and he weakly clutched where the bullet had torn through his abdomen. She could see the pain in Kevin's eyes as he ignored his own flesh wound to tend to his little brother. Erin's blood-slicked hands trembled as she clutched her jet black hair and wept uncontrollably. A long stream of blood trickled down her cheek from a gash on her forehead. Her young boy was nowhere to be seen. A chill ran down Karen's spine as she had a morbid thought. Had she passed by the boy's body and not even noticed?

The storm curtain parted abruptly, flooding the room with light. Another prisoner was callously shoved through the portal, skidding to a halt in the dirt as the curtain closed again. Jacob. He coughed and twisted his body in agony. Karen quickly moved to his side. She turned him over and cradled him as she inspected his wounds. Four gashes on his arm were caked with a mixture of blood and dirt. One eye was swollen shut, and he clutched at his ribs. If she had to guess, he had been beaten by their captors. None of this made sense. Had he fought back when they arrested him?

No, he wouldn't have. He's not like that.

"What happened?" she asked.

"Jack," he whispered hoarsely.

"Jack? What about him? Where is he?"

"He's dead." Jacob laughed. Soft, but maniacal laughter. "I killed him. And the others. I saved us all, Karen. I saved us all."

The pungent smells of wet earth mixed with the tang of the salt air. Gabi had forgotten her jacket at home, though she didn't really mind. She would be soaked from head to toe in just a few minutes, but the driving rain would be a blessing soon anyway. She looked up into the gray sky for a second, letting the cool drops beat down on her brow and cheeks. This was different than when she washed her face in the river. Somehow the rain always felt cleaner, and just a little warmer.

When the rains passed was her least favorite time. She could never breathe right for a few days after. The adults said it was the humidity in the air. All she knew for sure was that it felt like breathing through a moist towel that was tied too tightly around her mouth. One of the most important things she had learned from two years in Camp Eight was that the good was always followed by the bad, and the bad in turn by the good.

A terrible wrong had passed. It was time for the good. The evil invaders from Lake Raphael had been defeated, and the ones that Seth caught had been forced to bury everyone who died. And now it was their turn to be punished. She flattened herself against the earth and peeked through the tiny gap in the thornwood bush. Pepperine vines wove a tangled web through their chosen host plant, ensuring thick cover. It was one of a hundred similar places Gabi could hide within a mile of the village. Gabi wasn't supposed to be here. Will and Chief James would be upset by the thought of eight-year-old Gabi defying their orders to witness a punishment. Still, she knew that if she stayed still and quiet, none of the adults would know she was there.

After about five minutes James arrived with the prisoners. They approached from behind her, so all their backs were turned as they came to a halt twenty feet away. The prisoners were then turned to face the chief and his men, Seth and Troy. A rifle was slung across each of their shoulders. The three men from Lake Raphael had their hands bound together with tough palm rope, and two of them hung their heads in shame. The third kept his chin high. His face was grossly discolored; large purple and brown bruises dominated the left side of his face, circling his eye. His lip was turned upward in a sneer.

Gabi felt her temper rise. She wanted to run out of the bush and yell at James for making a mistake.

He didn't bring the right prisoners. He didn't bring their leader, Karen.

Gabi had decided that Karen was a witch of some kind. She knew it from the minute they first met. Witches were supposed to be ugly, and Gabi had thought Karen was ugly. She had pock marks and scars on her face and neck. Will had tried to tell her that they were burns from a fire, but Gabi didn't believe him. And she was right not to. Karen's people had brought the sickness with them. Then they murdered people. They murdered her new sister Kelly.

James had been furious that day. He screamed and shouted all day long. He threw supply crates, tore down the clinic's storm curtain with his bare hands, and even buried an axe in the wall of the Palm Palace. Gabi was sad that his daughter had to die before he could see that Karen was a witch. She was even angry with him for letting it happen. That anger threatened to boil over and send her running across the muddy ground to confront him, and to yell at him for not bringing her to be punished. But she didn't want to be sent away. She didn't want these men to go unpunished just because she couldn't restrain herself.

Instead, Gabi growled under her breath and clenched her teeth. It made her feel better, and she didn't think the adults could hear over the rain, since she couldn't hear them. She watched James talk to the three men for a minute, then he and his men took a few steps back and formed a line. They readied their rifles and aimed. Gabi covered her ears to prepare for the louds blasts, and closed her eyes.

Six shots followed in rapid succession. Even though Gabi told herself she wouldn't be scared by the gunfire she still flinched. When she opened her eyes, the prisoners were all on the ground, lifeless.

Good, she thought. *Maybe the witch is next.*

She slipped silently through the back entrance to the bush and made her way to the shattered pod, where she knew Will would be waiting for her. Gabi shook off the images of the executed men; those would come back to haunt her in her dreams soon enough. She needed to make sure she didn't keep him waiting too long, or else he would make her run twice as long as normal.

Motus Domi, Act I

```
Gov Darius Owens
5 July, 2 yal, 14:16
North Concordia
>|
```

Perfect, Darius thought as he leaned against a wall on the opposite side of the street, admiring the market square. A couple seconds later he heard a door swing open just a few feet to his right. The apartment's tenant stepped out and emptied a foul smelling bucket into a shallow gutter. The liquid slowly trickled along the engineered chasm, but the solid excrement just sat there, waiting to bake in the sun. *Well, almost perfect,* he corrected.

It didn't matter that he was upwind of the dump site. Much of the colony was cursed with at least a lingering odor of human waste. Hot days like this one were particularly bad. Other than the small biosolid processing facility onboard each sleeper ship, there was no sewage system in the colony, nor would there be for a long time. A system of trenches had been carved through Concordia, leading to pits in the ground covered by iron grates. But movement of the solid waste was glacially slow. Once the problem was apparent, and it was clear that the colonists couldn't build a sewer overnight, Darius was forced to enact an unusual, if not disgusting, solution. Sanitation squads, popularly known as "dung draggers."

The immediate (and obvious) jokes about Darius assigning a "shitty job" to those unfortunate colonists had worn thin just as soon as they had been made, at least as far as he was concerned. The uproar had died out months ago, though he still overheard an occasional sarcastic exchange made casually over a trade. He had come to terms with the fact that his title would always earn him at least a measure of disrespect. That's all that politicians back home seemed to reap, in any case. He just felt pity for the men who made up the dung squads. Their primary functions were to keep the streets of Concordia as clean as possible, transport the waste—including what was pumped from the pits—to the ships, and deliver processed fertilizer to the farms. It was as perfect of a system as they could provide without a sewer, but because of the sight and smell, colonists complained.

Darius shook his head and turned his attention back toward the chatter of the market square as he walked along the street in the opposite direction. Early evening was one of the busier times of day for the market. The vendors, who hours before had bided their time by tidying their shops, setting displays, or making their products, were now engaged with a steady stream of customers. Though negotiation played a heavy role in the transactions, the mood was very amicable, and friends and neighbors laughed and joked as business was conducted. This made Darius smile, and it was this sense of community spirit that prompted Darius to move his meager office from the bridge of *Gabriel* to *Michael* earlier in the spring.

The hardships of the winter seemed forgotten. The deaths of fifteen colonists were not, nor would they ever be, but they were no longer a dark blanket that suffocated the spirits of the people. Instead, they emerged from the snow and ice with a renewed sense of purpose, even if resentment for Darius still ran high. The intrepid pioneers had set their minds, bodies, and hands to work, and as a result the variety of available wares had grown significantly over the past year.

The drought of the previous year was not a repeat affair this time around. Brightly colored native fruits and leafy greens were sold alongside large ears of corn and sacks of flour, both products of Earth. Countless varieties of roots and tubers from both planets offered staple foods for every style of cooking. A half dozen refrigeration units and two freezers had been hauled from *Michael's* hold, and the market square had been tied into the town's power grid. Four of the refrigerators were installed at the grocer's to prolong the shelf life of some of their goods.

All of the remaining units, including the freezers, had been installed in the butcher's shop, two doors down. Wild game from the trappers and hunters was available here, along with meats from the odd farm animal that was turned in. The butcher, Frank Devereaux, was as shrewd as he was skilled with his cleaver. He traded in favors just as often as he bartered, and cashed them in with both his suppliers and his customers, linking woodsman and townsfolk without either having to come to an accord. He was, in essence, the colony's ultimate middle-man. And everyone loved him, too. Not just because he occasionally had bacon for sale—which was a rare treat—but because of his gift for putting people at ease. Darius figured that this probably played into his negotiating skills.

Darius casually crossed the street and sat on a wooden bench just outside Kimura Clothiers. This allowed him a better view of the neighboring butcher shop, and he focused his attention on a transaction that the Marine-turned-butcher completed.

First came the request from the customer. In this case, a whole gray pheasant, a native bird that was a little larger than a chicken, and less greasy when cooked. A whole bird was sure to be expensive, and Darius could only imagine the kinds of goods it would fetch in trade. Devereaux displayed the impressive fowl, but instead of starting off with price, he asked about the woman's family. The exchange was short but friendly. He then made a comment about her husband's work at the flour mill. She answered. He smiled and paid a compliment to her and her family. Then it was down to business. Darius tried to pay attention to the nuance of the situation, but he still couldn't figure out how he managed to secure two sacks of flour for the bakery around the corner, a home cooked meal for himself, and a favor to be cashed in at a later time. He did, however, notice that Devereaux quickly jotted something down in a notebook before moving on to the next customer.

So he has a way of tracking it all, Darius thought. *Like money in a bank.*

The web that the butcher wove was complex, but it looked like it all boiled down to tracking where debts of favor sat, probably cross referenced with known demands. Hook up the favors of a supplier to a client. Sometimes Devereaux was the client, but usually not. Darius yearned to spend time in the butcher shop learning Devereaux's secrets.

Maybe someday. Not today.

He let out a great yawn as he stretched stiff, tired joints. He suddenly realized how tired he was from a day spent touring Concordia from the irrigation channels to the River Islands, with what seemed like a thousand stops in between. A glance at his watch told him that it was rapidly approaching the bottom of the hour. It was about time for the sanitation squads to be making their rounds, though Darius couldn't hear the telltale sound of their crawler's diesel engine. He got up and was about to make the return trip to *Michael* when Devereaux called for his attention.

"Governor?" he asked, his voice carrying over the crowd. "Power's out."

Confused, Darius moved swiftly to the shop, craning his neck to see the refrigeration units in the back corner. "You sure?"

"Yeah. I just heard them all click off a few seconds ago. Normally they don't all go off at the same time."

"That's odd," he remarked.

"Frank?" The grocer, Kim, had come to investigate as well. "Your fridges work?"

"Nope. You're out too?"

Kim nodded. A mixture of irritation and concern crossed her face.

Darius scratched the stubble on his chin. "Alright, I'll look into it."

"Thanks, Governor."

Darius puzzled over the power issue as he made his way back to *Michael*, following the line of power transmission poles. With no buildings to shade him as he checked the poles, the hot afternoon sun soon had his brow dripping and his shirt stained with sweat.

What the hell could it be?

He had personally helped run the grid for the market square, and Novak had wired the buildings. Everything from the transmission poles to the refrigerators was less than a year old, and the main grid was two years old. He couldn't fathom what the issue with the power was. He checked the grid interface on the side of the sleeper ship from a safe distance, but everything looked good. Darius continued around to the rear of the ship. He was so preoccupied with running every diagnostic scenario through his head that he nearly walked past the crawler at the end of the ramp.

Darius halted in his tracks. The massive tank and pump in the bed of the crawler were unique to one function: the sanitation squad. It was not supposed to be parked at the end of the load ramp, but rather around the side, where the waste tank port was located. The crawler sat idle, and no one was in the cab. A split second later he heard chanting and shouting from inside the ship. Without another thought Darius charged up the cargo ramp and sprinted to the rear stairwell. He was out of breath by the time his foot hit the first stair, which he almost missed in the creeping darkness. But he pushed through the burning in his muscles that grew hotter with every hurried leap. He mounted the treads three at a time, nearly losing his balance as he shot to the top of the ascent. The only illumination came from two strips of emergency lighting in the floor.

Shouts of anger and declarations of victory echoed from the support section. Darius pressed forward, though the poor lighting and the threat of tripping over attachment points in the floor kept him to a brisk walk. The voices were definitely moving toward him, and he could make out bits of the excited conversation.

The pieces of the mystery all fell into place. The loss of power. The lack of regular lighting or humming machinery on the ship. Angry voices from the support section. Someone had seized control of *Michael* and shut down the reactor. There could be only one motive for doing something so drastic: to hold the colony's energy supply hostage. Darius froze in horror.

Shit, if they didn't bring the reactor offline the right way...

Civilians were prohibited from entering the reactor area for a number of reasons, not the least of which was the danger involved. Darius was shocked that this group would be so brazen as to violate that restriction. He cast caution aside and broke into a run. Darius reached the hatch to the support section and found it guarded by four men. The lack of light made it difficult to recognize them, but he figured that two were the errant sanitation squad. One was a wiry man who repaired machinery of all kinds. The fourth man was unfamiliar to Darius. Upon seeing him, they collected around the mouth of the airlock, barring his path.

"Let me get through," he demanded.

"Not a chance, Governor," the wiry man replied with a smug grin. "We control the power now."

"You won't for long."

One of the sanitation workers laughed. "Like you could get past us."

Darius tried anyway, and was easily pushed back by their combined strength.

"You don't understand," he said. His uneasiness came through in his voice. "You might have just shut down the reactor for good. Or worse, you could have started a core dump."

"So?"

"So?" Darius parroted incredulously. "So the reactor will go critical, and then what do you think will happen?"

"Nothing." Tyler Quinn's deep voice echoed through the darkness with his footfalls.

Quinn? What the hell?

The engineer emerged from the airlock. The other men parted to let him pass, quickly moving back to position once he was through.

"The reactor's been shut down properly," he continued.

Darius's fear of a reactor meltdown faded away, only to be replaced with anger at Quinn's actions. "You did this for them?"

Quinn shook his head. "I did it for Concordia. I only found out about the planned strike an hour ago. I didn't have enough time to warn you, so I came here to shut it down properly. I had Forrest shut down *Gabriel's* reactor, too." He paused for a second, seemingly waiting for a response from Darius. "You're welcome, Governor. You can go home without being incinerated tonight."

Darius just sputtered and stammered. He was grateful that Quinn took action to prevent a catastrophe, but enraged by the men who would risk everyone's life, or at least bring the colony to a grinding halt. Without power, neither the grain nor lumber mills could function. The foundry would idle, and the market's refrigeration would be compromised. Nearly everyone in the colony would feel the effects of this action. Perhaps not immediately, but at some point, like ripples on a pond.

"Turn it back on," he ordered.

"Not until our demands are met," the wiry man shot back.

"Demands? This is ridiculous! Do you have any idea how much damage you're doing?"

He was met with an impassive shrug. "That depends on you, Governor. I'm sure you're pretty steamed about this, so we'll wait until tomorrow morning before we present them."

Darius fumed, but decided against saying anything further. He knew that he was near the point of losing his temper, but that wouldn't help the situation. He was outnumbered and outmuscled. The only thing he could be thankful for was Quinn's intervention with the reactor, though even that still stung. He felt there was something more he should be doing to resolve the matter, but he couldn't think of what. The picketers had already determined they wouldn't yet present their demands. Hanging around for the townsfolk who still called the sleeper ship home was no wiser, as it was sure to draw unwanted attention to the strike. All Darius could do was retreat to the bridge to stew.

As he rested his weary body in his chair, he tried to think of how it came to this. He wasn't popular with the people, but his deputy assured him that no matter whether or not individuals agreed with his policies, they at least appreciated how difficult the decisions were. Now all of that was thrown out the window; there was at least one group in the populace that was openly defiant. He needed to know why. As Darius kicked his feet up on his desk and sank deeper into the chair, his heavy eyelids slowly losing their battle against fatigue, he decided that would be his first order of business in the morning.

* * *

J.C. Rainier

Silentio Martyrii

Karen Daniels
7 July, 2 yal, early morning
Camp Eight
>|

Light flooded the hut as the storm curtain parted momentarily. Three times a day for over two months, the brief glimpse of the outside world heralded the prisoners' meals. At first it took a half dozen trays to feed them. Then Jacob and the Morgan brothers were taken and executed, and only five trays showed up. As others died of their injuries or were executed, the number dwindled further. Now only one tray showed up, a tray large enough to feed both Karen and Erin. Not that the size of the tray mattered that much, as Erin barely ate at all. She spent most of her time curled up in the corner, staring into oblivion.

Her husband died of the plague. Her only child was murdered. What more does she have to live for?

The rhetoric was pointless. Erin had simply been surviving on instinct for the past month. Her body compelled her to eat even as her mind had shut out the world. No matter how much Karen tried to get through to her, she wouldn't respond. Karen would have stopped trying altogether, but after Rick finally succumbed to an infected leg wound, she kept talking to Erin. It seemed ridiculous to her at first, but Karen soon learned that the silence was driving her mad. Talking to a catatonic woman was better than not talking at all.

"Morning," she muttered to Erin. "Chow time."

Erin slowly drew her body off the ground and shambled to the front of the hut. She knelt down and blindly grabbed a piece of fruit and flatbread, then retreated to her corner and slowly consumed the food. Karen knew this was an automatic response; Erin would retrieve her food even without being spoken to. But announcing mealtime was one of the few threads of normalcy Karen had left.

Karen quickly finished her share of the breakfast, then slid the empty tray under the edge of the storm curtain. One of the guards on the other side pulled it through, as was routine. She returned to her roost, leaning up against the wall as she sat.

"Another day of the waiting game," she noted. "Will one of us kick it today?" Karen pondered silently. A slight, wicked grin crossed her lips. "Not likely. You haven't figured out how to die yet, and they still don't want to kill me."

Karen glanced over at her silent companion. Erin rested on her right side, and she seemed to be watching a particularly large beetle that was investigating some errant palm leaves on the floor.

"Still don't know why that is," Karen continued, picking at a layer of grime under her fingernails that never seemed to go away. "You'd think I'd be the first one they would have executed. Well, maybe after Jacob, anyway."

The conversation, as usual, was going nowhere. Karen shrugged and tore a long leaf from her mattress cover, then began to fold it inch by inch into a tiny accordion. She tried to remember the last conversation she had with someone on the outside. Something banal and insignificant, but she couldn't even remember who she was speaking with. Tran, the guard? Troy? She couldn't recall, no matter what. She sighed and closed her eyes, searching deeper for something she could remember. It didn't take her long, but it wasn't pleasant, either.

The stench of body odor cloyed the air, mixed with stale vomit. The Palm Palace never smelled the same after it was used as overflow for the clinic. The victims of murder and disease had long since been removed, but their presence remained, even if only perceptible to one sense. No cords bound her wrists, but Seth kept a watchful eye on her from the entrance as she approached Chief Vandemark.

The inquiry, she recalled through the haze of memory. *Two days after his execution.*

"You wanted to speak with me?" she asked, defiantly refusing to address him by title.

Hard eyes glared back at her. He wasn't an imposing man, so it was a little like being growled at by a Shih-Tzu. "It's time to tell me everything."

"Everything's a lot. And not very specific," she shot back. "Would you like me to start with my sixteenth birthday, or would you be so kind as to actually ask me what you want to know."

His brow furrowed, which did nothing to inflict fear in her. "Let's start with your lieutenant, Jacob. What exactly was he planning to do?"

"Did you ask him that yourself before putting a bullet in his brain?"

"Of course. Now I want to hear it from you."

She shrugged. "Then you should already know I had no idea that he was up to anything until the attack happened."

"Attack is a little soft of a word," James growled. "Your man slit ten peoples' throats in cold blood before he even left the clinic. Then he killed one of my scouts and started shooting in the middle of town square. What was he trying to accomplish?"

"I think he just snapped. He was going after the ill."

"Just snapped?" His expression was a mixture of rage and disbelief. "Just snapped and went around killing helpless, sick villagers. Your people, our people. Then stepped outside to what, have a smoke and murder the rest of us?"

She felt a flicker of anger rise within her. "You're acting like there's some sort of bigger plan here. Like he had some sort of scheme to overthrow you and take over your so-called paradise here. Like the fact that he was ranting like a lunatic afterwards was just an act."

"It makes a convenient cover for failure."

"And a convenient excuse to interrogate people. A little seed of conspiracy that you can tantalize your people with to make us the enemy, when we're just as much the victims as you are," she accused.

"Victims?" he roared. "Don't talk to me about victims. A hundred and fourteen people, dead. Thirty eight of them children, including my daughter. Those are the victims."

Karen took three steps toward him before Seth's iron grip caught her arm and kept her at bay. "Thirty of the dead are my people. A dozen children. We share this tragedy with you, but you won't lift a finger to help a single one of my people. I got the pleasure of watching one of my friend bleed to death on the floor of your little prison. You could have saved him." She glowered at him, and her tone was laced with daggers. "And what happens to anyone from Lake Raphael who wasn't rounded up by your son of a bitch jailer here?" She yanked her arm free of Seth's grip. "I wonder, are you going to round them up too and put them in the pen with us, or are you just going to let the jaguars do your dirty work?"

"That's enough!" he bellowed.

"Is it? How does it feel knowing there's probably some kid out there who's about to be something's lunch?"

"How does it feel to murder your own people?" James retorted with a snarl.

"I'm not the murderer here," she spat. "I've done everything you've asked since we got her. You're looking for shadows where there aren't any. There's no plot. No scheme. Why can't you understand that?"

"The Morgan brothers, for one. They were caught fighting their way out of the town."

"Because they were scared and wounded. Trevor took a shot from one of your men."

James shook his head. "It's been established that Kevin killed Jenkins, then took his weapon. Jenkins never shot his brother."

Karen glanced back at Seth. He didn't make eye contact with her, instead standing at parade rest, looking straight ahead. *You lying coward*, she thought.

"Because no one from Camp Eight would ever be mistaken in what they saw," she added through clenched teeth.

"I don't need aspersions cast on the honor of my men to know that your people inflicted as much damage as they did. Your other lieutenant, Mina, was armed when she was killed. Along with about a half dozen others."

"So?" Karen replied. "Most of the adults are armed. I don't doubt that a few of them shot back. You're a fool if you think they wouldn't have, or shouldn't have."

James waved his hand dismissively. "I've had enough. I see this is going nowhere. Feel free to come back when you're ready to tell the truth."

"So you'll let me go as soon as I tell you what you want to hear?" she mocked. Silence answered her.

Of course. How silly of me to expect that he would ever let me go.

Karen opened her eyes. The suffocating stillness of the prison hut soon began to press upon her, and she felt as if she needed fresh air. She moved to the doorway and drew the curtain back a few inches, letting in a rush of tangy sea air. She drew in a deep breath, reveling in the refreshment it provided.

Tran leveled his rifle at her. His hands trembled ever so slightly, and he seemed surprised that she would be so bold as to open the curtain herself.

"Back inside," he ordered.

Karen paused for a moment, catching a glimpse of a four-winged gull in flight. It twisted in the air, then dipped and rose in exaggerated movements. The gull seemed to be enjoying its freedom, something that Karen knew she'd never have again. She sighed, and turned to go back into the hut. But something stopped her.

"I want to speak with Chief Vandemark," she said.

Tran hesitated for a moment, then nodded. He led her at gunpoint through the town square, past two burned out huts, to a larger hut on the outskirts of town. She was shown inside, and James dismissed two men with whom he was conducting a meeting.

"To what do I owe the pleasure after all this time, Sergeant?" he said coldly.

She knew that the use of her formal title was a slight against her, but it was easily ignored. She was too tired of games to engage at that level. What Karen planned to do was unsettling enough, though she knew it was the only way she would get her freedom.

"Chief Vandemark," she addressed him. "I would like to make a formal proposal."

He regarded her incredulously at first, then burst out into laughter. "What could you possibly offer me that I'm interested in?"

"I could ask the same of you," she replied. The scowl returned to his face. "I've been locked up so long that I'm not even sure what I want is something that even exists. But I have to try."

"Alright. Let's get this over with." The passivity in his voice made her think that James had already rejected the proposal, even without hearing it.

"I'd like peaceful reintegration of any Lake Raphael survivors back into your village."

His hands froze and he blinked at her twice. "And what do I get in exchange for such an exceptional request?"

Does that mean there are survivors?

"My life," she replied.

"Now, you see, I already have that."

"Alright, let me be more specific. My confession and execution."

James slowly removed the beat up glasses from his face, then crossed his arms. He paced back and forth for a moment in silence. "And just what are you confessing to?"

Karen swallowed, forcing down her pride and indignation. "The plan to oust you from leadership and take over Camp Eight."

A wry grin crossed his lips. "I knew it. I knew that your man didn't just snap."

"Oh, he did," she shot back immediately. "I hate to crush your dreams, Chief, but there wasn't any actual plan. That's still all in your head. What happened was all just a horrific, tragic incident that got way out of hand in an instant. But if it helps my people at all, I'll say you were right all along. Then you'll finally have the right to kill me, just like you've wanted."

She could see his jaw grind as he nodded slowly. "You're dead whether I let you rot or you confess your sins." He paused. "Why now?"

"If there's anyone still out there, they need help now. And if not, then you can at least let Tran here go back to something more important than babysitting me." She glanced back at the young guard to gauge his reaction, which was rather confused.

"He'll still have to watch Erin."

Karen sighed and shook her head sadly. "She's already dead. Her body just hasn't figured it out yet."

"And just what am I supposed to do with her, then?" he grumbled.

"Not sure. She's your problem, though. As I understand it you had someone in a similar situation before. Didn't end too pretty from what I heard."

His brow furrowed deeply and a snarl formed on his lips. "Fine. I accept your offer. Prepare your confession, since you're going to be executed tomorrow. Now get out."

The truth stings, doesn't it, Chief? Karen took a small measure of satisfaction that she finally managed to inflict a wound on her arrogant opponent, even though it sealed the deal that would cost her life.

Tran escorted her back to the prison hut. Erin lay on the floor exactly where she had been left. Karen knelt over her and gave her a brief hug.

"Never let them forget your boy," she whispered in Erin's ear, reaching one more time for the soul trapped in the empty shell. "Never let them forget the truth."

Motus Domi, Act II

Slowly rubbing his temple with his thumb did little to quell the stress that seemed to squeeze tighter with each petition brought across his desk. His forefingers were firmly planted to his brow and his elbow was locked to the table. Darius drew papers one at a time from the thick stack in front of him, read them carefully, and put them aside. It seemed that every adult in Concordia was perfectly content to commit their grievances to paper.

This is just sick.

Bureaucracy was a special level of hell that Darius never liked, even though his title demanded it. The men who had shut down the ships' reactors must have known this, and they came up with the idea of allowing the townsfolk to bring their own personal problems up for negotiation. The past two days had been spent reviewing the submissions.

Initially, Tom and Darius tackled the problem with solemn determination. After the fiftieth request to do something about the sewage smell in Concordia, he knew there was a pattern. But then they reached a section of requests that were truly a bizarre, mixed bag. Requests for annual pig races. City-sponsored flower beds for every residence. Demands to name this animal or that the official colony mammal. Mandatory alien invasion drills. Creating a position where the sole responsibility was to wash the hulls of the ships. And those requests were some of the more tame ones.

But Darius had promised to read every demand, even if Tom felt they were being toyed with. It didn't help that in a number of cases an individual would submit both a genuine problem and one or more false complaints. Those were the ones that aggravated him the most. Now he was on the last stack of papers, and he could finally end the spiteful charade. Darius was able to pick out a handful of legitimate demands from the hundreds of complaints. As the last sheet passed from his hand into the completed pile, he ran through the list in his mind one more time.

Improve the sewage system. Improve the irrigation system. Increase the production rate of timber, stone, and iron resources. Have homes for every family built by the end of 3 yal. Enact mandatory colonial food stockpiling.

The last demand was the easiest to meet. After a cold, bitter winter that saw fifteen colonists die of starvation or exposure, the stockpiling programs that he instituted the previous summer had been credited with saving hundreds of lives. It was commonly acknowledged that without being forced to, the people would not have saved enough food, and the toll would have been unfathomable. Yet as the second full year on Demeter unfolded, some had resumed their gluttonous ways. It was possibly psychological in many cases. Darius couldn't fault those individuals; he had gorged himself once or twice when bountiful root and fruit harvests became available. Still, rationing might be necessary even in good years. There was no doubt that Darius would give in to this demand without an argument.

He leaned back in his chair to consider the other four, each of which posed a unique set of logistic issues. Tom arrived on *Michael's* bridge at that moment, bearing two plates of potato and pork hash. Fresh flatbread accompanied the main dish, still warm and moist to the touch as Darius tore a chunk and popped it in his mouth. Tom took his customary seat across the table. He pushed his food around with his fork, but didn't seem interested in it.

"Something wrong, Tom?" Darius asked. The deputy governor sighed heavily. "Don't tell me it's worse."

"It's worse," Tom replied, almost too quickly.

Darius slid his plate away from him and leaned back in his chair. Three days of complete work stoppages in the industrial district seemed to be a pretty hefty price so far. About half of the construction force had joined in the strike and refused to work, which halted progress of the housing demand. A handful of other colonists also joined their ranks. At least the agricultural community was adamant about not letting their fellow colonists starve by joining in the madness, and kept working as normal.

"How much worse?" he asked, almost afraid of the answer.

"We got word from Rust Creek this morning."

Darius closed his eyes and pinched the bridge of his nose. He could see where this was going. The miners and foresters of Rust Creek didn't exactly make social calls, and the timing was obvious.

"Striking?"

"Yup. The whole town."

And there goes our raw material supply. No iron. No lumber.

"Did they say why?"

"They did. They have a list of their own demands."

Darius opened his eyes to see Tom's hand outstretched, offering a single, folded piece of paper. At least Rust Creek wasn't playing games. Darius wouldn't need to spend an afternoon trying to find out what their real objective was. He took the page and unfolded it.

"Run the power grid to Rust Creek. Relocate the smelter closer to the mines. Build a market in Rust Creek," Darius read aloud from the page. He creased it between his fingers and looked up at his subordinate. "Power to their town? How serious are they?"

"Very. I met their representative myself. He said that they won't send another ounce of ore or scrap of wood downstream until they get what they want. No juice, no metal."

"They do realize that we have no power to give them in the first place, right?" Tom nodded. "And they realize that we won't have power until we get the building materials we need, right?"

The deputy nodded again. "It gets worse."

"How the hell can it get worse?" Darius growled.

"They don't want to deal with you directly. Something about not wanting to listen to a politician trying to spin his way out of things."

"Spin things?" Darius was floored. "What have I been spinning?"

Tom shrugged and sank deeper into his own chair. His voice was deflated. "Beats me. I had no idea how deep the resentment ran. Between the stunt that the dung draggers pulled off and what the miners are now doing, I'm starting to wonder if there's anyone left that still supports us. Hell, I'm surprised they haven't just yanked us off the bridge and given us the boot."

Darius didn't bother to object to Tom's usage of the sanitation squads' nickname. Had they not crippled the colony's power supply he would have defended them, but at the moment the label seemed appropriate. They were dragging everyone through the dung, and didn't seem to care about the consequences. But Tom was also right about something else. They could have just as easily had a coup on their hands, considering that several Militia officers were among the strike's leaders. The political damage already dealt would no doubt be felt on both sides of the river for years. But the more immediate damage was the delay of progress. Damage that the strike both caused and railed against. Just how much damage they were willing to inflict on the colony before their demands was met was anyone's guess.

That depends on you, Governor, he recalled the mechanic saying the night they cut the power.

It depends on me. They'll hold out forever. How long before the colony suffers too much? How long can the work stoppages at the mills go without jeopardizing everything we've worked for? His shoulders felt heavy as he let out a long sigh. *Can I even make enough promises to mollify them all? Or is this already the end of Concordia?*

He was suddenly aware that he had been silent for some time. Tom regarded him with silent concern, scratching at his ever-graying beard.

"We need some sort of response," Darius broke the silence. Tom nodded in reply. "And it needs to be one that will get their attention." He brushed his hand across the table, sending a flurry of paper flying. The release of frustration felt good, if unproductive. He sat back down and thought for a moment. "Obviously they think we're a joke, if they're willing to waste our time by shuffling their real demands in with the fakes."

"Obviously."

"Maybe we can use that to our advantage."

Tom returned a puzzled look. "How, exactly?"

Darius slid his chair forward, picked up his fork, and scooped up a bite of the hash. "Who's the one person you never hear anyone joke about?"

The deputy governor leaned forward curiously. "You think Devereaux's the key."

"No. Not Devereaux. Someone else that everyone knows and respects."

* * *

Why do you keep letting them talk you into this shit?

It wasn't the dozens of pairs of glowing, sinister eyes piercing through the night from both near and far that made Cal's skin crawl. It wasn't the calls of alien nocturnal creatures weaving through the dark stands of Demeter pine either, or the fact that his companion's lantern barely cut through the inky mantle that shrouded their path. What bothered Cal most was the memory of what happened more than two years ago, less than a mile from his destination. With every step the young mare took, the image of Elaine's gruesome death grew more vivid.

His body shivered involuntarily, as if another ghost from his past had reached from beyond the grave with icy fingers. An escort and a rifle were no match for spirits, imagined or real. He coaxed the mare to quicken her pace ever so slightly. Jake followed suit, making sure to keep just ahead of Cal in an attempt to return them to their previous pace.

"Something wrong?" Jake asked.

"Just want to get there before midnight," Cal deflected.

Jake was looking forward to spending the night indoors. He had not weathered the previous night's camping well. No matter how much Cal tried to convince his neighbor that reaper bears weren't nocturnal, he wouldn't calm down. This resulted in Cal spending much of the day leading Jake's horse along the narrow road with Jake slumped over, asleep. Cal credited him with having an abundance of balance. The uphill slope and rocks that jutted from the ground made the ride that much more challenging, yet somehow his slumbering companion managed not to fall off his mount once.

But with nightfall the trail had become downright treacherous. The upper reaches curved with the contour of the hills, climbing at a rate that the ore wagons could navigate safely. Erratic wheel ruts were cut into the dirt; narrower ones created by the wagons would suddenly flare into wide, deep holes where a crawler's steel treads chewed up the terrain, only to fade away into bare, flat patches where the terrain leveled off. After his mare had nearly thrown him when she stumbled on a rut, Cal decided it was best to ride at the shoulder of the road. Given the small equine population he was sure that bringing back a lame animal would be worse than failing his mission.

After fifteen more minutes, a familiar sound tickled Cal's ear. Bur-bling, babbling water greeted him from ahead, and the pungent smells of aquatic flowers and wood smoke filled his nose. To his companion this probably signaled a source of fresh water, a place where during the daytime one might take a break and reflect at the edge of the pond. To Cal it was an old wound. Again he spurred on his steed, trying to keep a step ahead of the gunfire that echoed through the years, and the visage of the snarling monstrosity that ended Elaine's life and shattered her family with a swipe of its paw. His effort to outrun the past nearly earned him a face full of pine branch, though he managed to duck just in time.

Why do you keep letting them talk you into this shit? He berated himself again.

Jake pulled up next to him. "Seriously, take it easy. We'll get there in one piece if you'd just stick to the pace."

 Cal clenched his teeth and nodded. He let Jake lead the way, though the pace seemed to slow to a torturous crawl. He relived every painful moment since his first trip to Rust Creek, before the settlement even existed. Elaine. Josephson's suicide attempt. Almost losing Alexis because he couldn't say no to Dayton. Cam's death. But the most ex-cruciating moment was when he relived the torture of watching Alexis nearly waste away from disease and starvation. It was a fear that Cal still clutched closely, despite the reports of bountiful harvests. And he was reminded of it every time he thought of his companion. The neighbor so desperate for food that he was willing to kill for it. The man who had never looked Cal in the eye afterward, much less thanked him.

Why did I pick him?

Cal knew the answer. Jake wasn't a negotiator, a bodyguard, or a statesman. He was there to paint a picture. Darius didn't understand Cal's selection of companion. The governor had given a half dozen alternatives who might be better suited for the task, but Cal refused them. Darius had expressed his grave concern, but Cal won out in the end.

Three soft, yellow lights winked in and out as trees momentarily eclipsed their view. The settlement that had sprung up near the bog ore deposits slowly came into view. Dark, square hulks loomed ahead of them as they approached, only recognizable as log cabins once in range of their weak light source. One particularly large building looked as if someone inside was still awake; its open windows were the source of the light, which danced and flickered.

"See? Told you," Jake chided as he dropped to the ground.

A few hitching posts stood in the dirt street in front of the building. They tied up their animals and Cal knocked on the front door. It swung open after a few seconds, and they were invited inside by a gargantuan, muscular, bearded man who seemed to have forgotten his shirt. Or possibly torn out of it. He wiped his meaty hands on his dingy blue jeans before offering one to Jake as a greeting.

"You must be the governor's negotiator," the man said. His speaking voice seemed to be as big as he was.

Jake winced slightly under the crushing grip on his hand. "Uh, no. That's him," he said, pointing to Cal. "I'm just along for the ride."

Cal stepped up and introduced himself, though the man's eyebrows arched quizzically.

"You?" he asked. "Governor Owens sent a kid to negotiate?"

So much for your plan to use my so-called fame, Governor.

Cal shrugged off the slight, though he did feel a little disappointed that his name apparently counted for nothing. The man showed them to their seats around a long, stout table hewn from rough planks. It was easily fifteen feet long and five feet wide, though the room easily swallowed it. A stone hearth jutted out from the wall behind the table, just about at the middle of the table. Neatly split logs sat to the side as others hissed and crackled in the lively fire. Tools of the wilderness trades neatly lined the near wall. The building was clearly some sort of gathering hall, though a dark opening in the wall at the far end of the table hinted that there was a small dwelling attached, possibly belonging to their host.

"Well, kid," the man started. "You're here, so you might as well get your part over with."

Cal's disappointment shifted to resentment. This man had requested a negotiator other than Darius, but then showed no respect toward the chosen emissary. He decided instead to stir the pot and play the same game.

"Alright, brick. Where would you like me to start?"

The man's eyes widened in shock for a moment, then narrowed as a sneer crossed his lips. "What did you just say?"

"Where would you like me to start, brick?" Cal said it as casually as he could, trying to suppress his satisfaction with the reaction.

The man's muscles rippled as he slowly stood up, leaning on the table with his knuckles. "You think this is a joke, son? Does Owens take me for an idiot, sending you here?"

"No, but you're sure acting like one."

"Cal, what are you doing?" Jake whispered, grabbing his arm.

Cal waved him off with a flick of his wrist. He rose, drawing the motion out to be even slower and more dramatic than his host's. "I'm serious in my intent to present Governor Owens's conditions, but you're not serious about listening. You called for me, not Owens, whether you like it or not. I have a name, and it's not 'kid'. You have a name, and I'm willing to bet it's not 'brick' either. But since you don't seem to want to give me your name or your full attention, it looks like I need to take the kid gloves off with you. No pun intended."

Hard, brown eyes stared back at him. Just as Cal was sure that his host would lunge across the table and mete out punishment for his insolence, the man gave a hearty belly laugh, and shrank back into his seat. "Now that's the Cal McLaughlin I've heard so many stories about. Fearless. Honest."

Unsure of what just happened, Cal took his seat with a measure of trepidation. "It's more reckless and idiotic. Not that anyone's counting anymore."

"Sometimes the only difference between the two is luck. My name's Norris. Welcome to Rust Creek, in all its glory."

"Thanks," he smiled weakly. "Where should we begin?"

"Your choice," Norris replied, gesturing his deferral with an up-turned palm.

Cal cleared his throat and took a second to prepare before he launched into the reasoned responses to the demands that the tiny community had made. He explained in detail why their request for a localized smelter was rejected due to environmental concerns, particularly those of possible arsenic contamination that could flow downstream to poison the city's water supply. He laid out the reasoning why a market could not be built at this time, mostly due to the population of the settlement being far too low to support such a venture. He projected a timetable for electrification of Rust Creek, the only demand which Governor Owens agreed to. All the while, Cal watched Norris's expression slowly sour until an indelible frown distorted his beard.

"I can see how this ends, Cal," Norris finally said after three excruciating minutes of silence. "We don't agree to your terms. The workers in town get what they want. We keep up our embargo of timber and iron to try to force the issue. Maybe you find a new source of timber, maybe not. But you then cut off our food supply to try to force our hand. Guess I should have my people out picking berries tomorrow, huh?"

Cal shook his head. "The townsfolk are only getting one of their demands met right away. We can't meet any other terms at this time. Besides, whatever you think of Governor Owens, he's not callous or vindictive. I don't think it ever crossed his mind to cut off any supplies from the town."

"But he will, sooner or later."

"He won't."

"I wish I could believe you, Cal. I really do."

"Believe it. Even if he goes insane and tries to cut you off, I promise I won't let it happen."

Norris shrugged. "I appreciate the sentiment. Doesn't change a thing for us, though." He stifled a yawn and stretched, his fingers nearly touching the rafters as he did so. "Better get some sleep, guys. You've got a long road ahead of you tomorrow."

"But we're not done here," Cal protested. "We don't have an agreement."

"You're right, but I wouldn't want to waste your time. Or mine. You can use my room in the back for the night. I'll see to your horses and gear," he said as he stepped out into the night.

Jake shot Cal an irritated look. "Well, that was worth the ride."

Cal knew that the mission was unlikely to be a success. That didn't make the disappointment of his failure any less bitter, or ease his racing mind as he bedded down for the night.

Calvin McLaughlin
The next morning, 06:17
>|

Cal yawned as he listlessly pushed the bland, gray mush that passed for cereal around the sides of his bowl. He formed it into tasteless mounds, then flattened them one by one with the back of his spoon.

"You're not supposed to play with your food, you know. Bad manners," Jake mocked.

"It's supposed to be bad manners to starve your guests," he fired back.

Jake shrugged. He made a sour face as another spoonful of gruel slid its way down his throat. "It might just be all they have for us. They don't have the luxuries that we have back home, like eggs or a neighborhood bakery." Jake proved his point by dropping his stale slice of bread, which shed large crumbs in every direction on impact.

Cal choked down the rest of his meal in silence. He wished for just a few leaves of rosemary or a wild onion to give the gray ooze at least some flavor. The bread was staler than what was left of the loaf he had brought from Concordia, going down his throat like tiny jagged rocks.

If this is all they've got, I don't blame them for striking. He sighed. *I just don't know what they're expecting to get. Darius is giving him the only thing he can.*

Norris burst through the door, though Cal supposed that a man of that size probably couldn't enter a room any other way. He had at least chosen to wear a thin jacket this morning, sparing Cal the sight of his barrel chest.

"Your horses are ready," he announced. "You can be on your way now."

Cal nodded, though his attention was still elsewhere. He kept going back and forth between the stale bread and his own provisions. It suddenly dawned on Cal that anything made in Concordia would not be fresh by the time it made it to Rust Creek. Bread was only the beginning. Fresh fish was an impossibility since none of the crawlers had refrigeration, so whatever they ate had to either be smoked or caught from the creek itself. Greens and other fragile vegetables might not survive the journey either.

Is that why they want a market? Do they want us to come to them? Was that just a power grab, or did they honestly think it would help their situation?

"What were you hoping to get at the market?" Cal blurted. The two other men looked at him in confusion. "If we built a market for you here, what kind of goods did you expect to be able to trade for there?"

Norris slowly walked to the chair next to Cal. The chair let out a soft creak as he straddled it and leaned on the back. "I don't know. Fruit. Vegetables. Household goods when they're available. I've been down to the city a couple times this summer and really admired the market square that you've built down there. I know we're just a tiny speck up here, but I thought maybe we could have a store that had it all."

Cal smiled warmly. "Did you stop at Devereaux's butcher shop?"

Norris laughed heartily, the same deep rumble that Cal heard the previous night. Norris broke into a story about how Devereaux wanted to know the personal business of everyone in Rust Creek. At one point Norris jokingly accused Devereaux of being a "horrible gossip", but was impressed by the man, his goods, and his fairness in dealings. Norris had walked out of town with a hen and rooster from one of the farms, and a sack full of Demeter pears. It turned out that Devereaux needed firewood, and Norris delivered. At the end of their dealings, Devereaux still owed Norris twenty favors.

"I'm not really sure what that means for us," Norris chuckled, "but it's got to be good, right?"

Cal laughed along with him, and Jake followed suit. "I bet you could buy a feast for the town for that much." The laughter died out and an uneasy silence followed. "So what happened to the chickens?"

Norris shrugged. "They didn't last long up here. The rooster flew the coop a few days after I came home and a reaper got it. The hen got freaked and wouldn't lay eggs, so she became dinner."

So the luxury he worked for before is already gone.

"You don't need a market," Cal added. "Without power and refrigeration you can't support a market like Concordia's. But what if we could give you something more useful in exchange?"

Norris's smile disappeared, but he nodded slightly. "I'm listening."

Cal leaned back, thinking about how he would word the proposal. Without warning, Jake spoke up. "Me. My family."

"What?" Cal gasped, sitting bolt upright.

"You?" Norris snorted. "You're worth a whole building?"

"By myself? No. But my family's worth a lot to you. Maybe I could convince some others to come with us."

"We don't exactly have space for you," the lumberjack pointed out.

"Just hear me out." Jake paused to make sure he wasn't going to be interrupted. "My wife is a hell of a cook. I've been working in the mills. Now I know you don't have any up here, but I'm not afraid of hard work. Anything you can think of around town that someone's doing right now, I can take over. Or you can send me to the mines if you need me there." He snapped his fingers and he smiled. Whatever idea was working its way through his brain had to be giving him pleasure. "I've got it! Chickens and fresh veggies. Maybe some herbs, too. I can make a little garden up here. I bet with that spring so close by, it'll be a snap."

"Now hold on, son," Norris butted in. "You're talking a mile a minute here. This isn't at all what we asked for."

"Maybe not, but it'll have the same effect," Cal added.

"Oh? How do you figure?" Norris's arms crossed, and he regarded his guests skeptically.

Cal proceeded, undeterred. "Think about it. You were impressed by the market, and one of the things you came home with was a pair of chickens. That didn't last long the first time, but if you had someone tending a flock the whole time, maybe the results would be different. And imagine having fresh bread to go with your eggs, not the stuff that's stale by the time it makes it up here from Concordia. And trust me; I've eaten Cora's food. She's a better cook than my wife, and that's saying a lot."

"Alright, so what if he can tend chickens and his wife can cook. You're still not offering a lot. Besides, we take care of each other up here. Not sure the others would be keen on taking in a strange family. Not like this."

"Then you don't know how much a hen is worth," Cal retorted, laughing nervously.

Jake's reaction was the opposite; his expression hardened, and his tone took on a sincerity that Cal had never heard before. "We take care of each other, too. To the end, no matter what."

Norris locked his gaze on Jake. "Then how did so many people down there die last year when we didn't lose a single one?"

"Sacrifice." The response was immediate and unwavering. "We sacrificed for each other. When we were starving and cold, we sacrificed our own supplies for our neighbors." Then his words turned bitter and accusatory. "Did *we* miss sending a single ration shipment to your village?"

Norris shrunk away, knowing the answer already. "No."

"Then don't think for a second we're any more callous than you." Jake looked at Cal and nodded once. "That we'd leave our neighbors to suffer."

In that instant, Cal understood the real meaning of Jake's outburst. It wasn't anger at Norris for demeaning his offer. It was gratitude for Cal's selfless act the winter before. An act that had nearly raised the death toll to sixteen, with how close Cal had come to death's door.

The silence that followed was brief, but in its own way, it spoke volumes. Even before Norris confirmed his acceptance of the new conditions, Cal knew that his neighbor had turned the negotiations around. His neighbor had sacrificed his life in Concordia, cast his die to live in an even smaller town, and saved the settlement from a protracted strike. But even this struck Cal as bittersweet; Lexi was about to lose her best friend.

Principium Novus

Any minute now, he thought, anxious about how his decision would be received. Having to come to the decision without involving Troy in the process was not something that James relished. Charlotte Bryant had been known to be a tenacious champion for her students, a quality that had become less of a boon and more of a liability in recent days, and her husband was still an esteemed member of the village council, the only remnant of Haruka's original staff other than himself.

James sat on one of the empty aluminum crates that served as chairs for the makeshift classroom within the Palm Palace. He wrung his hands together and ran the speech he had prepared through his head several times, paying keen attention to points that he would emphasize. He knew the exercise was futile; Charlotte would probably start tearing into him after the third or fourth sentence. It was solely for his sake, a small bit of habitual order he carried with him from Earth. The preparation ritual did its job, and he felt the edge of his nervousness dull somewhat.

Charlotte arrived exactly at the expected time. She kept her back straight as an arrow, keeping her tiny daughter from spilling out of the makeshift sling that carried her. Charlotte stopped in her tracks as soon as her eyes adjusted to the room's darkness. She looked around in confusion, perhaps trying to find out if the children were playing a trick on her.

"Where's the class?" she asked.

"Reassigned," he said, casting his speech aside entirely. His preparations meant nothing in the face of her anger, which was immediately apparent from her deeply furrowed brow.

"What do you mean by reassigned?"

"I mean we need them to grow up a little quicker than we'd like. With how few adults are left breathing and able-bodied, we don't really have a choice."

"You can't be serious," she grumbled. "I can see maybe letting Karina and Kris…"

"I've given each child their assignment," he continued, ignoring her protest, but taking the time to stand and meet her condemning stare. "They will apprentice with an adult to learn useful skills…"

The agitation in Charlotte's voice was growing stronger, and she continued to talk over him. "Useful skills? They're just children. We can't have them running around the village or the forest like lumberjacks or…"

"…That I feel are best suited to their personality and knowledge base," his voice escalated over hers. The volume of their argument was making it difficult to make himself heard without shouting or letting his temper slip.

"Jesus, how can we build a future if we don't let our children learn what…"

"What skills are useful?" he finally snapped, bellowing over her voice. "In case you hadn't noticed, we need people that can keep food on our plates and roofs over our heads. It's a grand notion that you want to give them the kind of education that you or I could get on Earth, but it's just not realistic."

Her nostrils flared wildly, and he could tell that her teeth were clenched. Daphne stirred at the escalation in noise, and began to whimper from inside the sling.

"I'm reassigning all children who are at least seven. You can stay on to teach the younger children, and to prepare them for the apprenticeships they will eventually receive. Otherwise you can pick up a saw or a shovel and get to work."

"So you're going to make kids like Gabi or Marya pick up a shovel too? Is that it?"

James narrowed his eyes, and his lip curled into a sneer. "You know damn well what Gabi's been up to since you banned her from your class-room. I found something a little less dangerous for Marya. You can at least thank me for that."

"Troy's not going to like this. When I go home and tell him…"

"Troy has about as much of a choice as you," James said, slowly walking past her. "Keeping those kids cooped up in this room might just be the straw that breaks the colony's back. It might make the difference between them starving and surviving." He paused briefly at the storm curtain, giving her one last thought before he departed. "I know you don't like the idea. I don't like it either. We're just out of options. There aren't enough of us left. We'll need another teacher in the future, and I hope like hell we can let Daphne apprentice under you. That's the only silver lining I can give you."

And I truly hope I can at least give you that, he thought as he left the Palace.

* * *

J.C. Rainier

```
Gabrielle Serrano
7 September, 2 yal, early afternoon
In the jungle, about 2 miles from Camp Eight
>|
```

Gabi traced the depression in the dirt with two fingers, noting the depth and curvature of its edges. She dabbed at the pool of water that had collected within, trying to figure out how long the rainfall would have taken to fill the hoof print to that level.

She glanced up at her mentor. "An hour?"

Will chuckled and shook his head. "You still don't have a good grasp of time. That print's about ten minutes old."

She growled in frustration. She was trying her hardest to learn the tricks that Will was teaching her, but it was hard. Gabi could tell that they were tracking a long-tusk boar, but the age of the tracks threw her off every time. It didn't help that the weather on the island had been so erratic, either. One day it would be pouring rain and the next would be chokingly muggy as the burning sun came out. She wanted to throw her vinewood bow in frustration. After all, what good would it do her if she was never allowed to shoot it at an animal? But Will insisted that she carry it while they went hunting, even though he was the only one who ever fired his weapon.

"Which way did it go?" he asked.

Gabi looked at the pattern of the tracks. They meandered around the base of a pepperine-shrouded tree, then to another. She slowly walked the path that the animal took, noting its habit of only visiting areas where pepperine plants grew. She gently took a sheared off stalk between her fingers, examining the shredded end carefully. Her stomach growled as the sweet odor of a half-eaten pepperine wafted into her nose. Gabi pushed aside the complaints of her empty belly.

"This way," she pointed deeper into the jungle. "It was here to eat."

"Good," Will nodded. "Let's go."

They followed the tracks to the edge of the river, where they again appeared to jumble in an almost random pattern. Gabi knelt down in the middle of the trampled dirt, trying to discern which way the animal had gone. Freshly disturbed soil near the river's edge made Gabi think that the boar had been digging for tubers, which were plentiful near the slow moving river. It was also a common place for animals to drink.

If it stopped, we can catch up with it.

"This way," she pointed upriver, confident in her analysis of the boar's trail.

"And we're only a couple minutes behind," Will noted as he dabbed his finger into the water pooling in the tracks.

They hurried off again, nearly as fast as Gabi could run. It was difficult for her to keep up with her older companion on the narrow game trail, but someday she knew she would be able to match him stride for stride. The conditioning and training he had already given her allowed her to run for almost twenty minutes straight, though they never needed to.

A couple minutes later Will pulled up to a halt and crouched down at the top of a short ridge. Gabi crawled up next to him, looking down into the dense thicket below. Will pointed into the gnarled vines, but she could not find the beast.

"It's right there," he whispered. "Don't you see it?"

"No," she whispered angrily.

"Give it a second."

Will's index finger tracked slowly left. She was just about to smack his hand and rebuke him for lying to her when a brown hump of fur appeared in the sea of leaves. The boar moved slowly; it was apparently unaware of their presence. Or at least unconcerned by it. The animal grunted as it searched for something.

"Your turn," Will grinned.

"For what?"

He reached to the quiver on his back and slowly drew an arrow. She could tell at once it was too short for his bow. Gabi's eyes widened as he passed it to her.

"Me?" she gulped.

"You've got to learn sooner or later."

Her heart raced and the tips of her fingers tingled. Gabi slowly and quietly stood up, making sure not to startle the animal. She nocked the arrow and squared off, slowly and deliberately bringing the weapon to bear. Her right hand trembled as she pulled back on the string. The bow creaked ever so slightly as it bent to her will.

"Now remember what we practiced," Will said in a hushed tone. "Extend and tighten. Extend again, then tighten. Aim down the shaft of the arrow. You'll need to aim a little high at this distance. Not too much. Thumb steady, and let your fingers go to release the arrow. Just your fingers; keep your form or your shot will wander."

Gabi could feel her fingers twitch as she drew the arrow back and her thumb brushed her cheek. Suddenly an idea crossed her mind, and she saw the boar as the mother of tiny baby boars. She wondered what they would do without their mother, and if the cruel jungle jaguars would hunt them down quickly. She paused, then dipped her bow down and slowly relieved the tension on the string without firing.

"What's wrong, Gabs?"

"I can't do it," she replied. "What if it's a mama boar?"

"What if?" Will replied callously.

"Then her baby boars will starve and die."

Will nodded, but his expression was unchanged. "They probably will. Or they'll become prey for something else. What does that matter to you?"

"I can't kill the babies' mama!" she protested.

"I can understand that. So we walk away. Then the jaguar on the other side of the hill kills it anyway. Then what?"

"Then I'll go find the babies!"

Will laughed softly, pinching the bridge of his nose as he shook his head. "First off, you'll never find them. Second, I don't even want to know what you plan to do with them."

Gabi's cheeks flushed and she felt her temper flare. "That's not funny. Babies deserve to have their mamas. They can't live without them."

Suddenly her mentor's expression turned hard. "They can't, huh? Well, you are. Your mom's gone, and you're still here."

She growled and swung the bow at him, which he easily avoided. "I'm not a baby!"

"If we were back on Earth you might still be called a baby by some people. You're surviving. Wild animals lose their parents all the time to predators. Some of the babies survive, some don't. But I guarantee you that a jaguar doesn't care if that boar has kids. All it cares about is satisfying its hunger. It kills and it eats, or it dies."

"I'm not a jaguar," she insisted.

"Not yet." Will quietly gained his feet and nocked an arrow in his own bow. "But you're hungry. I can tell. The question is how hungry."

"Not hungry enough to kill a mama!"

"Shh," he hissed, sensing a change in the animal's behavior. They froze for a moment to make sure that their prey did not scare off. "We'll find out if that's true. Sorry it's come to this, Gabs. If I hit it before you do, you don't get to eat tonight."

"What?" she shrieked, sending the boar tearing out of the thicket and over the far hill.

Will lowered his bow and sighed in exasperation. "Great. Now we have to track it again. Thanks."

"I'm not going to shoot it. And it's mean to take away my food if I don't. I'm telling your dad."

"Dad's on board with this. You need to learn a lesson here. We're all just animals at this point. We do what we have to do to survive. Or we starve."

Will stalked quickly along the top of the ridge, his bow at the ready. Gabi found it even harder to match his pace with a nocked arrow, so she unloaded her weapon to pursue him. He did not go very far, stopping on the ridge over which the boar disappeared. She found it facing them, pawing for a charge, tail straight in the air. Will glanced at her only once as he raised his bow.

"Remember what I said. I meant it."

The gnawing pangs in her stomach had grown worse. She could only imagine how terrible they would be later in the evening if Will kept his word. Gabi had gone hungry for a night before, when the adults were too busy burying and weeping over the bodies from Karen's massacre to feed the children. She was about to face that same tormenting pain again, and it was because of her unwillingness to take an animal's life. This animal was nothing like the fantasy of Pelusina, her stuffed cat that she had magical dreams about. This was prey, and dangerous prey at that.

Long-tusk boars always raised their tails before they attacked, and she had once witnessed one gore an adult jaguar, spilling its innards all over the jungle floor. This boar was squared off to Will, and it was only a matter of seconds before it would spring into action. Not because it wanted to kill Will. Because it was threatened. Terrified.

Gabi set her arrow in the nock and raised her bow quickly. The muscles in her arms and shoulders complained as she drew back the string, tightening as she aimed. She was too late to beat Will, as his loosed arrow flew from his bow in a blur. The pit of Gabi's stomach dropped, but not because of the realization that she had waited too long and lost her dinner for the night. Will's arrow missed its mark. His aim was ever so slightly off, and the tip of his arrow glanced off of the boar's tusk just an inch from its face.

The boar's powerful legs went into action at once, propelling the

J.C. Rainier

beast directly at Will. He shouted a curse and reached for another arrow. Time seemed to speed up, and Gabi had only a second to react.

If I had to aim high when it wasn't moving, I need to aim high and in front if it's moving.

Gabi spun a little to her right, leading the target with the arrow. She had almost no time to aim before she let loose the arrow. The palm vine string sang as it snapped back into place. The arrow arced slightly before coming down into its target. Gabi's aim was off as well, and the arrow found flesh far to the rear of her intended target, sinking into the haunches of the beast. The boar squealed and its hind quarters dropped, dragging in the dirt.

The delay was enough. As the boar found its feet again, Will's second shot plunged into its chest, and it collapsed in just seconds. Though gravely wounded and screaming at the top of its lungs, the prey continued to thrash. Will drew another arrow and fired again from as close as he dared get, and the boar finally expired. Gabi circled it, look-ing into its dead eyes as its tongue drooped from the side of its mouth.

"You'll be happy to know," Will noted, "it's not a mom. This one's a male. And you've definitely earned your dinner."

She took in the sight of the chipped, cracked tusk that protruded from the left side of its mouth. This animal was no mother. That was all something she had imagined, and it almost cost Will his life.

I'm not a little girl, she thought. *I can't act like one anymore. I have to be a jaguar.*

Viae Duas Vitas

Calvin McLaughlin
24 December, 2 yal, 15:03
North Concordia
>|

Pale orange flames flickered and danced over the logs in the fireplace, filling the air with crackling sounds and pungent smells from the pot of rabbit stew that hung above the fire. Heat rolled off in waves, cutting down the bitter chill of the room. Cal rubbed his arms underneath the blanket that draped over his shoulders and smiled. Three days of work during the waning days of summer, spent patching gaps in the rough timber walls and river rock chimney, had yielded a dramatic reduction in the building's draftiness. While still cold, it was nowhere near the previous winter's bitter chill that sliced to the bone.

Alexis padded over to the fire, stirring the pot with a long, wooden spoon. "Just a few more minutes," she chirped cheerfully.

"Time for a wood run, then," he replied as he glanced at the nearly empty spot on the floor next to the stairs where they piled their firewood. Only two slender pieces and a few scattered scraps of bark remained. Goose bumps rose on his skin as he shed the blanket, and darted downstairs. He peered into the darkness under the covered shed out back and considered spending a few minutes splitting more wood, but thought better of doing such a task. Instead, he went to the storeroom and loaded a bundle of cut firewood into his arms, retreating to the loft above to unload his burden.

Alexis had portioned the stew into two bowls already. She sat at the foot of their mattress, staring at the mesmerizing flames as she dipped a chunk of stale bread into the steaming brown broth. Cal carefully added a piece of alder to the fire and joined her, once again shrouding himself in the warm fur blanket. As he ate he watched the flames lick at the newly added fuel. The log hissed and crackled; not exactly the driest wood, but it suited the purpose.

That fire reminds me of something, his doppelganger's voice interrupted him. The unwelcome intrusion startled Cal, and he almost choked on a searing hot carrot.

"Are you okay?" Alexis asked. He nodded in silent reply.

Go away, Cal snapped back at the voice, irritated.

Don't get snippy with me.

Cal felt a hint of indignity from his alter ego. This only aggravated Cal more. He clenched his teeth and stirred his stew, trying to ignore the interruption. It was some sort of psychotic personality break, as

Dr. Taylor had explained it, caused by his hibernation on the journey to Demeter. Psychological side effects of the sleeper berths were rare, but the research crew had known about them before the ships ever left Earth. The clinical term was "Hibernation Psychosis." Cal simply referred to his irritating mental delusion as "Jerk."

Dr. Taylor had recently discovered that an anti-psychotic medication could be synthesized from a combination of native plants, and it worked well in suppressing Jerk. Unfortunately a steady supply of the medicine was not available during the winter, and it had been three weeks since Cal's last dose. His unwanted friend was paying him a visit more often, sometimes being enough of a pest to disrupt his chores.

"I was thinking about how sad tomorrow will be," Alexis said softly.

Ooh, I love it when she brings this up, Jerk giggled.

Cal took another bite of the savory stew. *And I hate it when you interrupt her. Shut up and go away.*

"Why's that?" he replied casually, careful so as to not tip off the argument in his head.

She sighed heavily and frowned. "Because they're not going to be here for Christmas dinner."

Cal slipped an arm around Alexis and drew her close, kissing her on the forehead. "I know. But they can't just come back for a day and go back. Not in the middle of winter."

"But there's so much space on the ships," she protested.

"I know. But it's too far for them to travel without a crawler, and you know that Traci's not going to go pick them up."

Alexis bit her lip and nodded. Her chin drooped, and she stirred her food aimlessly.

Boy, she's pissed with you, Jerk noted.

Me? Why me?

Because you sent Jake and Cora away.

It was Jake's choice.

Feeling Jerk's amusement was an odd sensation, like shame mixed with enjoyment. What made Cal's skin crawl was that at times he could not distinguish his own emotions from those of his alter ego. As much as he wanted to suppress the tingling sensation of glee, he could not do so completely.

What? Cal asked.

Sure. Their choice. Right after you came home from a critical negoti-

ation, sent there by Darius.

We've been over this, Jerk. She understands their decision.

And I still think you're blissfully ignorant.

God I wish Dr. Taylor had more medicine.

Oh, but then who would keep you sane? Jerk quipped.

Cal dug his pinky into his ear and rooted around, as if he could remove the voice if he tried hard enough. This only made Jerk laugh more.

"I wonder what it'll be like for them up there," Alexis mused as she finished off her meal.

Well, Jake won't be sticking a gun in my face, Sweetie, Jerk interjected.

"Oh, they'll be fine. Cora's going to have her work cut out for her whipping up the feast they're sure to have. Hopefully Jake can keep Norris out of her hair. And everyone up their loves the kids, so I think they'll be happy all around."

"And not missing us," she added sadly.

He put the bowl down and wrapped his arm around her, pressing her warm body against his. "Of course they'll miss us, Lexi. But that's their new home now. Besides, if we somehow managed to go up there, you know that Doc would be disappointed. And I'd never hear the end of it from Hunter."

She gave him a cross look, though it barely masked her amusement. "Oh, and I'm supposed to be worried about you getting your ear chewed off by Hunter?"

"Hey, it's not as much fun as it sounds. And you know what they say. Happy husband…"

Alexis cut him off with a playful shove. "That's supposed to be happy wife, dork. How would husband even rhyme with life?"

"I'll find a way."

She squeezed his shoulders, then collected her empty bowl and stood up. Cal knew she would be demanding his dishes in a moment, so he wolfed down the last of the chunks floating in the thick broth, then soaked the liquid up in his bread before handing it off. She went downstairs to clean up while he relished the remnants of his dinner.

Smooth talker, Jerk noted. *You're already forgiven.*

Told you she wasn't mad.

Oh, I know her better than you think.

Cal smirked. *Well she doesn't know you at all. Doesn't that make you a stalker? Yeah, I think so. So you just made your creepy level go off the chart.*

Irritating Jerk was a minor victory for Cal. Though the shared bond with his specter would inevitably transfer a sliver of the pain and resentment, the satisfaction he felt was well worth the cost. Cal enjoyed several minutes of silence, staring into the fading fire before adding a log and stoking the flames. He was beginning to wonder where Alexis was when he heard the unmistakable squeaks of the fourth and fifth stairs.

She returned with an enameled steel cup in each hand. She offered one to Cal before returning to his side. The steaming liquid that filled the cup nearly to its rim smelled of spice and alcohol. He took in a deep breath, savoring the vapors and building anticipation for the first taste. He nearly scorched his tongue in his eagerness to try the concoction, but he could distinctly taste cinnamon and Demeter pear. He had never tasted such anything so smooth, yet flavorful, and he found it difficult to remember the last time he had alcohol.

Three days after your wedding, numbnuts.

Thanks, Jerk.

I'm always here for you.

I was afraid you'd say that.

"Do you like it?" Alexis asked, trying to contain her enthusiasm.

"It's amazing! What is it?"

"A little something special," she grinned, holding her cup out for a toast. "Merry Christmas."

He tapped his cup against hers, and they both drew a short sip. "Merry Christmas."

"Frank owed me a few favors," she explained. "So I cashed them in. This is from the first bottling. There's a guy on the south side of the river who went a little overboard with collecting wild pears this summer. He couldn't give them to the canning crews fast enough before they started to go south, so he made cider out of the rest. Just a limited run. Frank got his hands on a case. I'd hate to think of how much the guy owed to give up something so rare."

"Wait, I heard about that brewer guy. What's his name again, Mitchell?"

She shook her head. "No. Mitchell is only doing beer. This guy just did it as a side project. His name starts with a D. Dante, Dameon, something like that."

Dingus, Jerk tossed out at random.

Shut up.

"Well, it's really good. I mean, that little kick of cinnamon makes it taste like…" Cal's voice trailed off as he tried to find the right word.

"Home. Christmas. That's what I was hoping for when I traded for the cinnamon."

"So you're going to go into debt with the whole town to make an ass-kicking drink," he joked. "Do you think Frank takes souls in trade? Because I'm going to want another."

She chuckled, then told him the story of how she came across the items and was able to negotiate for them. He was mildly shocked to find out that she had bid some of Cal's biodiesel as the bulk of the payment. He inquired about what Devereaux would want with the fuel, and she spun off into a story about how Devereaux and the other merchants in the square had collectively purchased a small diesel generator from the colony's supplies just before the start of winter. She relayed Devereaux's plan to keep business running uninterrupted for the bulk of the year, and to have an emergency power supply in the winter should nature turn against the fragile power infrastructure. By the time the tale had finished, Cal was draining the last few drops of his beverage. His head was swimming slightly, and his limbs tingled with warmth. He yawned and stretched contently.

"Didn't mean to keep the old man up too late," Alexis joked, knowing that she was seven months older than him.

"Really," he chortled. "You feed me that wonderful dinner and try to get me drunk, then you expect me to stay awake? I'm only a man."

Cal set their cups on the dresser as she settled under the thick reaper bear blanket. He turned the blazing log, exposing a small, hot pile of embers, then added one last chunk of wood. He retreated under the covers with his wife before the log caught and the fire flared up cheerfully. She stroked his cheek as he looked into her emerald eyes, a place he frequently got lost.

Should I close my eyes now? Jerk mocked.

I'd prefer it, pervert.

You know you're talking about yourself, right?

Cal sighed. He began to wonder if selling his soul for another drink would be wise, or if he should sell it to Dr. Taylor for more medicine. Having his alter ego hanging around during intimate times was not in any part of his plans, but he had to deal with it.

"Do you think we've finally made it?" she asked softly.

"Hmm?" Cal wasn't sure what she meant.

"The town. The colony. Do you think we've made it yet?"

He shrugged. "We've had a rough ride so far. I think we're all finally working in the right direction. Together, this time. I guess as long as the planet doesn't throw us any more curve balls, we'll be fine."

"What about us? Do you think we've made our way here in the colony?"

Dude, Jerk perked up instantly. *Red alert.*

Shut it.

Fine, ignore me. I won't help you out any more.

Like you've ever helped, Cal muttered mentally.

"I think we've weathered a lot, but we're still here. Nothing's going to shake us, right?"

Cal could feel Jerk's amusement, though he pushed it aside.

Her lips turned up in a shy, heart-melting smile. "I'm just glad you're back and settled in." She bit her lower lip and gave him a hopeful look. "You are settled in, right? No more running off?"

"Believe me, I'm done with running everyone else's errands."

Yeah, she's heard that before.

Shut. Up.

Fine. Fine. I'll go away.

I've heard that before.

"And you're finally at peace? You know, with your work situation?"

Cal smiled and brushed an errant lock of hair into place behind her ear. "More than happy with it. I'm hoping to expand next year. More than just diesel and soaps."

"Oh?" her eyes lit up.

"I've been tossing around a few ideas. I don't want to get into it too deeply until I know whether or not it will pan out. I should know more this spring."

"Well, that's good." She wore a smile, but something in her eyes said that she was hiding something from him.

"What about you? Are you settled in?"

"Yeah." He could tell by the way she glanced away that she wasn't being honest.

Cal cupped her hands, which were trembling. "C'mon. What is it?"

"I want more," she admitted. "I want what Cora and Jake have. What Jaime and Beth have." She must have read the confusion in his expression. She took a deep breath. "I want a baby. A family."

Cal's jaw dropped open, but not even the hiss of air came out. His fingers went numb in seconds, and he felt a great weight pressing on his chest. In an instant, he regretted every moment he had hidden his sickness from her. Every time that he had an impulse to confess the presence of Jerk but silenced himself for fear of how she'd react now came back to him, hammering him repeatedly with the realization that once again he had failed her by not admitting the truth. He steeled himself for the taunting that Jerk was sure to give him. But it never came.

What the hell just happened? Jerk asked, his own confusion piling on top of Cal's emotions. There was a brief, though very awkward pause. *Oh for the love of God, if you've never listened to me once, listen to me now. TALK. TO. HER.*

"I ah..." he stumbled.

Oh shit, Jerk added, though oddly it was out of sincere concern, not mockery.

Alexis tore her hands away. Her lips quivered, and a single tear rolled down her cheek. "Guess I have my answer."

"No, wait!"

"It's cool," she said as she rolled over, turning her back to him. "We can talk about this after you settle in with your expansion."

Oh, this hurts my head so much.

Shut up.

Gladly. I don't think I can stomach this.

"Wait, where's this coming from?" he asked. She answered him by rolling the blanket tighter around her shoulder. "No, serious, Lexi. This is all news to me, and so sudden."

Alexis propped herself on one elbow, facing him once more. Tears were flowing from both eyes, and her eyes burned like green flames under water. "Why is it that your wife is always a second or third thought to you? Why is it that anything I say or want is so sudden? Was it too sudden when I told you on our wedding night that I wanted a child?"

"I thought that was the whiskey talking..."

She slapped him in the face before he could finish the sentence. "You never think. You never ask me. You just go off and do things. Things that you want, or worse yet, things that other people want from you. But never what I want from you."

Cal rubbed his cheek, which still stung from the blow. "Then why didn't you bring it up again?"

"Because I was too humiliated. Then last winter came around. I wanted to ask again, but we both got so sick. You were there for me. You cared for me. I knew how much you loved me, but I couldn't ask then, not when you almost died. Then the spring came, and we both got busy with work." Alexis let out an enraged growl. "God, I don't even like what I do anymore. All I want to do is stay home with you, help you run your business, and have a family. You get what you want, but I guess I don't."

"Look, Lexi," he reached out for her. She slapped his hand away.

"Don't say yes. Don't do it because you feel sorry for me or because you're guilty. I don't want that. Just… just don't. Don't touch me, don't look at me. God, I hate you!"

He felt a stabbing pain deep in his heart. She was hurt, and lashing out in any way she could. Cal refused to believe that she hated him, though the anguish she was in was what really tore at him.

"I hate myself too. I did this to you."

"Oh, don't play that card," she groaned, her voice shaky.

Cal could feel his throat knot up, threatening to crush his voice. "It's not a card. It's the truth, and it's because I've been hiding something from you since… well, since before we got to the planet. Since I put you back in stasis after waking you up."

Alexis's eyes widened in horror. "Oh no. God no, have you been cheating on me?"

"What?" he gasped. "No! No, it's just…"

"Tell me, Cal. Tell me the truth, or so help me I will throw you down the stairs."

"I've got serious mental problems," he blurted, trying to get the words out as quickly as possible.

"No shit. But you still have to tell me."

"I did," he shot back, trying not to give in to the frustration welling up inside. "Just let me explain." She looked back at him, nostrils flaring, staring daggers, but silent. "There's a rare condition that develops in some people when they're in biostasis for a long time called Hibernation Psychosis. Doctor Taylor told me that it can show up as any number of mental problems. In my case, I have a rather obnoxious voice in my head."

Hey, I heard that, Jerk protested.

Alexis wiped her eyes. Her expression went flat, making it hard to gauge her reaction. "That's it? All this is over a voice in your head?"

"If it was just a once or twice thing, no. But sometimes I see him. He's me, only not. And he draws me into conversations."

"So, schizophrenia then?"

Cal shook his head. "Not quite that bad. Though some days it feels like it. No, he mostly hangs around to bully me and piss me off."

Meh, you needed that. Without me pushing you, you'd still be trying to figure out what to do. Or you'd be a bear's lunch. One or the other.

"And you couldn't tell me this for two years because?"

"I didn't want to scare you off. I couldn't lose you."

"Or you're just making this shit up to get off the hook. If that's the case, you've already lost me. I'll go see Darius about a divorce."

The thought of divorce was like someone hammering Cal in the gut over and over. Though he was telling the truth, he couldn't bear the thought of Alexis leaving him anyway.

"You want proof? You'll get it tomorrow, when we see Doc. She can tell you everything."

Alexis snorted, "Yeah, that'll make great dinner conversation. Hey, Doc! How's the new grandkid? Oh yeah, and is my husband nuts? Please, tell all our friends who are gathered here for a nice meal just how cuckoo he is."

"If that's what it takes to prove it to you, then let the whole world know," he replied without hesitation. "But then will you believe it's the truth?"

"A truth you couldn't trust me with. The one person you should never be afraid to confide in. Do you know how much that hurts me?"

"I do."

"No, Cal, you don't." She heaved over on her side, once again turning her back on him.

He sighed and ran his hand through his shaggy blond hair. "You're right. I have no idea how much I've hurt you since we met. I guess it's too late to fix my mistakes. All I can do is promise to be better. Can we at least talk this through in a couple days? Let our heads clear?"

"Fine," she mumbled coldly. "Good night."

He settled in to bed, though she balled up tightly in the blanket when he tried to touch her. Cal was left alone with his thoughts for hours. Just as the last of the fire's dim glow faded into darkness, Jerk returned with one final thought for the night.

Merry Christmas, numbnuts.

J.C. Rainier

Hunter tugged at the loose gloves on his hands, adjusting them so his fingers didn't bind when they flexed. The thin coating of slush on Benedict Boulevard squished under his boots as he hurried along. Giant flakes of snow drifted lazily down, adding to the wet, gray ooze that coated the city streets, and melting only moments after landing on his long, heavy wool coat.

He reached the door of the butcher's shop, the rapping of his knuckles muted by the leather gloves. Hunter waited for a minute, but his call was unanswered. He pounded again, this time with the palm of his hand. After a few seconds, Devereaux answered the door, draped from shoulders to toes in a fur blanket. Thin cotton socks peeked out from under it; Hunter figured that the man's feet were probably freezing, so he asked if he could come inside. Devereaux nodded.

They climbed the stairs to the sparsely decorated apartment above. Devereaux returned to his seat in front of the fire, offering one to Hunter. He politely declined, opting instead to shed his gloves and warm his hands at the hearth.

"This is an unexpected visit," Devereaux said, running his hand through his unwashed hair in a vain bid to make himself presentable.

"It is, and I'm sorry for that. I need a True Favor."

Devereaux nodded. "Straight to the point, I see."

Hunter had never shied away from asking for help, nor would he reject a friend in need. His trip to see the butcher fulfilled both ends of the spectrum. He knew he would be asking a lot. While the merchants traded in goods and favors—which had quickly morphed into a form of currency in Concordia—a True Favor was something special. It had no monetary value. True Favors could not be transferred from one merchant to another. They were a pact between the party that needed help and the person giving the help, who would then hold all the power. Hunter was hoping that Devereaux wouldn't issue a voucher against him, but it was a sacrifice that he was willing to make for his friend.

"Do you still have any more of that cider left?" Hunter asked.

Again the butcher nodded, this time very slowly. "One bottle. I was planning on saving it for New Year's."

Damn. That's going to cost me.

"Might I have it, please?"

"Anything's possible, Mr. Ceretti. I'd like to know why you need it so badly that you're asking me for a True."

"Well, first of all, because I don't think I could pay you enough favors to sell it to me."

"Obviously," Devereaux noted.

"And because it might just heal a wound. One that really needs healing, that I don't think I could bear to watch fester anymore."

"Alcohol doesn't heal wounds, son. Trust me on this one."

Hunter waved his right hand dismissively. "It's not the alcohol. It's the symbolism. It's the fact that it's Dante's cider. And it's this," he said, pulling a slim stick of cinnamon out of his pocket, grasping it between his index and middle fingers.

Devereaux's eyes widened slightly, and he nodded in acknowledgement. "It breaks my heart too, Mr. Ceretti."

Hunter returned the spice to his pocket and turned to face the butcher. "Then you know?"

"I can't avoid knowing things about people. Not in my line of work. I heard that the whole thing was a mess, and that they made a huge scene. Scared Doctor Taylor's grandkids. I'm sorry that your Christmas dinner was ruined."

"Thank you, sir, but the dinner's not important. I just want to save their marriage."

Devereaux's chair creaked as he lifted himself out of it. His feet made soft scraping noises as he shuffled to the window, pulling aside the small curtain and looking through the slats. "Do you think it can be saved at this point?"

"Not without a gesture," Hunter sighed, his friend's predicament weighing heavily on his heart. "That's Cal's only hope. I mean, he's good with them, but he's working with nothing right now. She's already threatened to move back onto the ship."

"I know she would, too. I don't know, maybe it's the pissy old Marine in me, but I would have already if I were her." Devereaux turned around, leaning his back against the wall. His arms were folded across his chest, somewhere underneath the blanket. "If this was back on Earth I'd probably say that he's getting what he deserves, she could do much better, all the usual shit we used to tell each other to make us feel better about our decisions. Out here everything's different. Call me crazy, but I think that the idea of them losing each other would be like a little piece of Concordia dying."

"It's worse than that for me, sir. It's watching two of my friends dying. Dying a slow, agonizing death from the inside. I can see that she still loves him, but she's so hurt that… well…"

The butcher raised a hand to cut him off. "I know. Downstairs in the refrigerator. I know it looks empty as you walk by, but it's hiding in the bottom out of sight. I'm not going to ask for a voucher on your True."

No voucher? Hunter almost tripped over himself on his way to thank Devereaux and shake his hand. *No voucher, and a True Favor. This is more than I could have hoped for.*

"I just hope you're right about Cal's gestures," Devereaux added. "For all of us."

Hunter took his leave to retrieve the bottle of cider which, true to Devereaux's word, was hidden in the lower corner of the refrigeration unit. He withdrew the cinnamon stick from his pocket, and tapped it on the glass.

How much magic do you have left in you, Cal?

Pax Concordia

Darius sighed, leaning on the cold, steel rail for support. Tiny rivulets of rainwater streaked the bridge canopy, and a dreary haze beyond shrouded Concordia. He could still make out the market square, though only barely. The rest of the town had been swallowed by the fog, as had the mighty Fairweather River. No one would visit him today unless they had to, and he had no particular desire to journey to town. He was alone, marooned and isolated by the confines of his temporary office and the weather.

The two hundred thirteen colonists that still claimed residence in *Michael's* sleeper pods were at work, and the children at school. Their absence was felt keenly, as if the very essence of life faded from the air when they left every morning. It was odd, Darius thought, that the man who was supposed to wield the most power in the colony would feel the way he did; like a dog waiting for his master to return at night. But for all that he had been through, and despite harsh words from his critics that made him wonder if he was wanted by the people at all, he still anticipated their return at night.

He wasn't sure why he still felt that way. Darius had no close friends among those left aboard. He had issued living quarters in the city to both Tom and Roger. The Kimuras were among the first to move out of the ship, and even Dr. Kimura had left before the first winter fell, forgiven by his daughter for the grievous sin of saving her life. He should have every reason to want to walk away from the constricting metal walls.

So why do I stay? He cast a glance toward the stairs at the end of the bridge. *Why don't I just take a stroll? It's not really that cold outside. Sure, it's a bit wet, but that shouldn't keep me here.*

Darius sighed and slowly shuffled to his familiar chair, brushing his fingers across the smooth aluminum surface of the folding table that served as his desk. He reminisced briefly about the hours spent hunched over reports, the countless meals taken in solitude when his subordinates were tending to matters elsewhere. It suddenly dawned on him that his administrative duties were dominating more of his time than he had realized. And as the days passed and seasons blurred, this isolation of his was growing as well.

I need to get out. I need to be around people again, not cooped up in my office. He sighed heavily and leaned forward, spreading the reports out with one hand. *But I can't just abandon my office. It'd take weeks to get Tom or Roger prepped to do my job, and for what? A week out and about? A trip to Rust Creek?*

He slowly paced back to the railing. The fog had lifted somewhat, though the drizzle continued to soak the landscape. Much of the vegetation between the ship and the town had been trampled and torn up from the seasonal camp that hosted those who did not yet have a home. They would file out of the ship and set up as soon as the weather turned pleasant, and return to the confines of the ship as fall blew into the wide valley. In their wake, spring rains turned the field to thick mud and wide, shallow puddles. It was the same way across the river, in the span between *Gabriel* and South Concordia.

Darius closed his eyes, recalling the vibrant grasses and lush flower shrubs that dotted the land around *Gabriel* in the weeks following the ship's landing. The contrast to how the field looked now was stark and appalling.

Even in this short time I see how much damage we have done.

His eyes snapped open as an idea coalesced in his mind. If left alone, the field in its current condition might take years to heal, given the disturbance to the soil. Eventually it would be repurposed for building something or another in the colony.

So why not speed that up? Let's do something with it. Something grand, something everyone can get behind. But what?

The answer didn't come easily. He postulated a number of possible uses for the land. A community garden might appeal to some, but be perceived quite differently by the farming community. Warehouses were too mundane and wouldn't inspire anyone. He even briefly entertained the laughable idea of starting a zoo, though he figured that would be too ambitious for the fledgling colony. The solution was both simple and complex at the same time.

Our heritage and our future. On this planet.

Why is he calling me up?

Frank cinched the laces on his boot tightly and double knotted them. He paused for a second, noticing a small smear of mud on the boot. He grumbled, spit on a rag, and wiped the offending blemish away. It was a futile gesture, since he was about to walk across a muddy, torn field to report to the governor, but the habit was deeply ingrained in him. Satisfied that his footwear was as clean as he could get it, he retrieved the small grooming mirror that he kept in his dresser. The man that stared back at him was not what he expected, given the context of the situation.

With every passing year, Frank's hair slowly grew grayer. At first it was a few strands, but after a few stressful winters, distinct patches of silver streaked his sideburns. The full head of wavy hair that accompanied those sideburns was also unusual. He knew that he hadn't been as rigorous about visiting the barber lately, but it seemed that his mane toned down his otherwise strong chin. He had at least had time to shave, which helped. But the image did not match his expectations for what he should look like in uniform.

As the leader of the Colonial Volunteer Militia, he was the first man to be presented with the new dress uniform. It wasn't something that Governor Owens had planned, but rather a gift from the Kimuras. Frank had only worn it once; when he received the wool garments from their creators. The ankle cuffs of the long gray slacks rested just on the top of his boots, and the matching double-button coat was trimmed in dark blue at the neck and cuffs. His rank insignia—two bars—was attached to the right side of his collar. This detail was another in a line of minutiae that made him question the identity of the man staring back at him in the mirror. After all, the Frank Devereaux that left Earth should have three chevrons on his sleeve, not bars on his collar.

Frank sighed and returned the mirror to its spot, then picked up the loosely curled note from the top of his dresser, unfurling it to read once more.

* * *

CAPT DEVEREAUX –

YOU ARE HEREBY SUMMONED TO THE BRIDGE OF
MICHAEL AT 0800 TOMORROW MORNING FOR A MATTER OF
COLONIAL INTEREST. PLEASE MAKE ALTERNATIVE
ARRANGEMENTS FOR OVERSIGHT OF YOUR BUSINESS, IF
NECESSARY.

THOMAS DAYTON
DEPUTY GOVERNOR
CONCORDIA

He rolled the paper up tightly, clenching it in his left fist. The note was vague, as communications from the governor's office often were, particularly after the previous year's labor strike. It wasn't a surprise to Frank, either. The idea was to slow down gossip about projected plans until after the appropriate meetings had been conducted. It wasn't something explicitly drawn out by the government either; it was simply what Frank had concluded after countless conversations in the course of his business.

This was different, somehow. Perhaps it was because Frank had never been summoned before, or because the wording of the note made it clear that he was going as a member of the Colonial Volunteer Militia, not as the town's leading businessman. He slipped on a thin jacket before heading outside into a light drizzle.

A hundred questions ran through his mind as he trudged through mud and grass, his stiff leather boots squeaking softly on the uneven ground. *Michael* loomed ahead, its gray paint streaked occasionally with rust. The ship seemed even larger and somehow alien as he approached. Nerves didn't often get the best of Frank, but he was keenly aware of how unusual everything felt, even if he couldn't point a finger at the source of his apprehension. The torrent of thoughts was only broken when the squeaks of his boots changed to a soft clank as he boarded the ship.

The governor's liaison, Roger, met him at the base of the bridge. The once-lieutenant greeted Frank and took his jacket, directing him to the conference table on the bridge. Frank climbed the treads with measured steps. Saika Kimura sat at the table with the governor, who rose to greet him, though his face contorted in confusion as soon as he saw Frank. Frank was just as shocked to see the younger Kimura, as she didn't often venture from the market square or its comfortable social circle.

"Captain, I hope I didn't disrupt any Militia exercises by calling you here today," Owens said.

"Sir?" he asked, waiting otherwise silently for permission to sit.

"Your uniform. I wasn't expecting that."

Frank looked down at the note, still rolled up in his hand. "Sir, the deputy governor's summons. He addressed me as Captain Devereaux."

Owens paused for a moment. The corner of his mouth twitched, like he was trying to stifle a laugh. He motioned to a seat across from Saika. "Probably a misunderstanding. You're here as one of our foremost business leaders. I also thought that your professional relationship with Miss Kimura would be useful if my proposal advances."

Frank nodded as he took his place at the table. "And just what proposal is that, Governor?"

Owens slid a piece of paper across the table. As it settled, Frank could tell that it was a crude map. He recognized the market square along one edge and the sleeper ship on the opposite edge, but lines and boundaries in between were unfamiliar to him. He glanced up for a second to see Saika crane her neck, inspecting the scrap in front of them.

"This is Concordia's next big project," Owens said. "I've already spoken with a number of people about it, including Deputy Governor Dayton, counselors Hausner and Abernathy, as well as representatives from South Concordia. There have been some good questions about the project, its management, and resources, and I'd like to get your feedback as well."

"What exactly is it?" Saika asked.

"A new civil complex." The governor walked around the table and pointed out what each delineation on the map represented. "This building across from the market will be a civic hall. It will contain government offices, as well as a public meeting hall. The area just to the west of it will be a park, dedicated to our heritage and future. Among other things I'd like to see a memorial to the *Raphael* disaster, as well as a tribute to the other ships. The land behind it is a little bit trickier. I'm open to suggestions."

"What's been thrown out?" Frank asked, searching for his own ideas at the same time.

"Community garden. Extension of the park. Playfields for the children."

"Playfields?" Frank retorted. "Don't you think that the drainage and grading necessary for that is a bit beyond what we're capable of at this time, Governor?"

"Possibly. I'm merely listening to all options."

Frank considered the possibilities that had already been suggested, as nothing new had come to mind. "I like the other ideas for different reasons, but I think a garden might be a bit more than we can maintain right now. So many of us already work seven days a week, and nobody works fewer than six."

Saika chimed in next. "What if we used plants that didn't require as much upkeep?"

"Like what?"

"Trees. What if it was an orchard?"

Frank nodded in agreement, while Owens pursed his lips.

"I've got consultants from the agricultural community coming in later today for a meeting. I'll see what they have to say about it. I may not be a farmer, but I grew up in Atlanta. I do remember that peach orchards take quite a bit of work to keep up."

The governor scribbled some notes on a fresh piece of paper. A brief silence fell on the room. Saika was still very shy outside of the merchant's circle, so Frank knew she probably would not bring up any new points of her own.

"Has a project manager been chosen?" Frank asked.

"Yes."

"Who is it?"

Owens set his pen down and folded his hands together. "Me."

"You?" he repeated, incredulous. "What about your duties as governor?"

"I've come to the realization that I've been underutilizing the deputy governor and his talents. He will be sharing my work load."

At that moment Frank experienced a conflict between his business instincts and those of his military training. Although he wanted to ask what the governor's impetus for such an unusual decision was, he felt that it wasn't his place to ask. After a couple minutes of silent deliberation, the business side caved in, admitting that it was probably neither his problem, nor relevant to the task at hand.

"So you mentioned that you believe that Saika and I can assist you. What's your vision for that partnership, Governor?"

"Excellent question," Owens replied. "The cornerstone to the heritage park will be the monuments. I need connections to make that happen, and unfortunately that's something I don't have. Two things are needed for this part of the project: resources and artists. That's where each of you come in. Miss Kimura, her mother, and their friends are the artists of the colony. You are the man who can get his hands on anything. If you're teamed up, you could procure any materials that Miss Kimura's team needs."

Frank again nodded, digesting the information. "And what do we get in return for our participation?"

The remaining excitement on the governor's face vanished in an instant. He leaned back in his chair, remaining silent.

"You don't have any way of paying us, do you?"

"Truthfully, no. I can always investigate the matter, but this project is for the public. Something to inspire the people and solidify our resolve."

Unity, he thought. It was one of the tenets of conduct so passionately delivered by Colonel Dayton at the Unification ceremony almost three years earlier.

"Keep talking," he said softly.

"You know how much we've all struggled, Mr. Devereaux. The cost in blood, the tears that have been shed. How we feel anger and joy, frustration and victory as one. This can be an example of that." Owens paused for a second, his mouth hanging open as if reluctant to go further. "And I know that you understand. I've talked with Hunter. He told me what you did for the McLaughlins. Their road is still rocky, but you have done the right thing, and helped them find the road. Honor and Unity, my friend."

"Honor and Unity," Frank repeated. He rose from his seat and approached the governor, who met him at his level. With a firm handshake, he added, "To the end, I will help you see it through."

* * *

Aqua Vitae

"Where do you want the rest of this stuff?" Hunter asked, hoisting a small cargo crate out of the back of the wagon. He dismissed the driver, who prompted his horse to move on to their next delivery.

Cal carefully shifted the bulky copper pot in his arms, making his way around the side of his shop. "Back here with the rest of the equipment."

They unloaded their loads under the shed. Cal positioned the base on of top one of his two large electric burners. Other pieces of the column still lay scattered around. Hunter opened the crate and excitedly handed various tubes and other small bits to Cal, who examined and pieced them together like a puzzle. It took about a half hour of discussion, argument, and profanity before the device was assembled.

"There she is," Cal beamed with pride.

"So are you going to tell me how you managed to buy this thing?" Hunter asked. "It's certainly unique, and I didn't think there was that much copper to spare. Not with Devereaux snatching it up to make bronze for that statue. And the glass? Small fortune right there, I bet."

Cal ran his hand over the surface. Small divots and waves gave the top of the pot a slightly distorted look. "A little insider secret I know."

"Yeah?" Hunter pressed, his curiosity piqued. "What's that?"

"Devereaux's already got all the copper he needs. They scaled back the size of the actual statue itself. Most of the monument is now going to be made of stone."

"Hah. Getting his leftovers on the cheap then?"

Cal sighed. "Not all that cheap. Fifty percent of the profits for five years."

Hunter shrugged, unfazed. "At least it's not fifty percent in perpetuity."

Cal forced a weak smile at Hunter's joke. Sometimes the dry humor that his friend used failed to hit its mark. Others found it charming or hilarious, but Cal didn't always get it.

"So where's Lexi?" his friend added.

"Out getting supplies for the first batch."

"Figured out what you're going to make?"

Cal began to disassemble the still, inspecting the parts to make sure they were clean, and preparing it for its inaugural use.

"I was thinking brandy at first, but it would cost an arm and a leg for the wine to make it. I guess it's up to Lexi and what she brings back. I'd like this to be as cheap as possible. Both for myself and my investor," he jerked his head toward the new equipment, alluding to his debt to its maker.

"Still, it'll be another first for the colony. You've had a couple of those now."

Cal looked up, puzzled by the tally of another claim to fame. "I'm not the first one to make booze. That went to Mitchell. Then Sandy, and then Dante."

"Beer, wine, and cider. You're the first to make liquor," Hunter grinned.

I still don't count that as a first, he thought.

"Well, I'll be known for biodiesel before anything else."

Alexis rounded the corner of the building, throwing up her arms in a dramatic shrug. She was covered nearly from head to toe in mud and dust. An impish grin crossed her lips. "So are you boys going to play with Cal's toy all day, or is someone going to help me unload the wagon?"

Cal planted a quick kiss on her lips as he passed. "Thanks, babe."

When he laid eyes on the bounty that his wife had provided, Cal's eyes nearly bulged out of his head. The wooden wagon's load platform threatened to scrape on its iron shod wheels under the weight of dozens of burlap sacks, each stretched and straining to contain their load. Oval lumps dotted several of the sacks, and at once Cal knew that Alexis got her hands on a significant cache of potatoes. Other sacks were smooth, likely full of grain. He eagerly hoisted the first sack over his shoulder, nearly toppling over backward from the weight. Hunter, Alexis, and the wagon's driver all pitched in, making short work of the load. By the time the sacks were stacked under the shed's roof and the driver dismissed, Cal's shoulders burned and his muscles ached, and his shirt was soaked through with sweat. He dropped to the ground, leaning against the treasure as he regained his breath. The whole time, a smile graced his lips.

"You did great, Lexi," he remarked, kissing her again and caressing her shoulder. "I saw the potatoes. What else did you get?"

"The only grain I could get anyone to sell me was barley," she panted.

"Can you use that?" Hunter asked.

J.C. Rainier

Cal nodded. "Think so. I'll have to do a little more digging, but I think that can be made into whiskey."

"Whiskey needs barrels to age."

"I know. Let me worry about that."

Hunter wiped his brow and looked at the sun, which was just about to rise into the obscuring overhang. "I know what the potatoes are for. Don't forget me when it's ready to drink."

"You get the first bottle, Hunter. I promise."

With a smile and a bow, Hunter departed.

"So here it is," Alexis said. "Your big expansion that you were talking about. Potatoes, barley, and an ungodly expensive piece of metal. So what are you going to do about barrels? Or storing it all?"

"I've got a couple feelers out on the barrels," he replied. "Storage was easy. Dayton is letting me use two of the empty cargo pods on *Michael*. It's a bit of a drive, but the price was right."

"Do I even want to know how much?"

He chuckled, knowing that she would appreciate the bargain just as much as he did. "Free."

She turned and looked at him as if an extra head had sprouted from his shoulder. "Free?"

"Yep."

"Why would he do that?"

"What else would he do with the space? Ship's almost completely empty now. And it saves him trying to figure out how to build a warehouse on top of everything else he's got going."

"And Darius is alright with this?" There was a hint of apprehension in her voice.

Cal shrugged. "He's already promised to honor any plans that Dayton makes in his absence, so it's not an issue. There's only one real issue left for me."

"Yeah? What's that?"

Cal stood up, pulling her up with him as he drew her close. "Are you ready to quit your job and help me out full time?"

Alexis hesitated barely a second before she whispered her reply. "Yes."

* * *

Hunter eyed the green swing-top bottle carefully. The handwritten label stated its contents in simple, bold handwriting. Liquid settled to a line just above the bottom of the neck. No bubbles or impurities could be perceived, though the unusual color and slight imperfections in the bottle's uniformity could have hidden something. He picked up the bottle and slowly turned it in his hand.

"Are you going to try it, or are you just going to stare at it all day?" Cal asked mockingly as he tidied up the display shelves in the front of his store.

"Sorry," he replied, setting it back down on the sales counter, next to an enameled steel cup. "I'm not used to seeing vodka in anything but a clear bottle."

"I promised you the first bottle. I didn't have a lot of choice in color or shape, you know."

"I know." Hunter pressed against the swing mechanism, and the cork popped off and away from the mouth in a precise motion. "Have you tried it?" he asked, pouring what he reasoned to be a shot's worth into the cup.

Cal nodded, though his nose wrinkled slightly. "I wasn't a fan. Neither was Lexi. Too strong. Not really sure what I did wrong, though. I thought I did everything that the book suggested."

Hunter brought the rim of the cup up to his nose and swirled the liquid slightly. He could smell the alcohol vapors, though not much more distinctly than products from Earth. "You said this is unfiltered?"

"Yeah. Didn't have any way to filter it. But I made sure to compensate for that with the still."

Here goes.

He tipped the cup back and swallowed the vodka in one smooth motion. Almost instantly his mouth and throat began to warm. It was by far not the smoothest liquor Hunter had consumed in his life, but it was surprisingly drinkable. He had been on a few microdistillery tours back on Earth, and the product that Cal had created was strikingly similar to a well-respected outfit.

"Give it to me straight," Cal said with a deflated sigh.

"Wow, that's really something."

"Too harsh?"

"Uh, not exactly," Hunter said. The warmth spread through his stomach, and the tips of his fingers began to tingle pleasantly.

Holy crap that's powerful.

"Not in the way you think," he continued. "I'm sure that stuff will kick my ass if I have more than another shot. It's disturbingly…"

"C'mon," Cal huffed impatiently. "Just get it over with."

"Accurate."

Cal joined him at the counter, a puzzled look scrawled across his face. He picked up the bottle and looked at it intently. "Accurate?"

"Yeah. I've had a few unfiltered vodkas before. I have to say, you're a quick study. This tastes almost as good as the pros back home."

"The pros," Cal echoed. "I'm trying to *be* a pro. That sounds like I missed."

"For a first try, I'd say you nailed it. You'll get better as you get more batches under your belt." A soft knock at the door distracted them both for a moment. "Don't stop now. You're definitely on to something," he added as Cal went to answer the door.

Hunter took another shot as Cal held a brief discussion with the caller. His head began to swim from the alcohol almost immediately. He capped the bottle, this time focusing his attention on the neatly handwritten label. Then his attention was abruptly called away from the spirits, interrupted by a low rumbling noise. Cal beamed with pride as he rolled a brand new 15-gallon barrel into the middle of the shop floor, putting his foot on it to pose.

"Guess who just sealed the deal?" he beamed.

Hunter set the bottle down and immediately knelt next to the barrel. He ran his hand along the length of one of the staves, admiring the smoothness that was only broken by the iron hoops, and noting the light blue distortion that rippled along the wood's length.

"Demeter blue elm?"

Cal nodded. "Properly charred. The closest thing we've found to white oak so far."

"And how much did these cost you?"

His friend grinned. "Much less than they should have."

Hunter whistled as he exhaled. "You must be half Devereaux."

"Maybe. But the *real* Devereaux is waiting for his first shipment of vodka. Can you give me a hand?"

"Only if I get to try the whiskey when it's ready."

Cal chuckled under his breath. "I hope you're a patient man. You won't see that for another few years at least."

"Of course." He clapped Cal on the shoulder as he went to the storeroom to retrieve a crate. "But for now, it's time to make you a prosperous man."

"Prosperous is a long way off. Debt free is my goal right now."

Hunter nodded in silence as he helped load the wagon.

I guess that explains how he was able to expand so quickly. Foolish, in my opinion, he thought. *But too late to do anything now but support him.*

Dedicatio

Thousands had gathered for the official dedication of the memorial and park. The new Civic Hall was open to the public, and Roger was busy giving tours to those who wanted a glimpse inside the new government offices on the second floor. The market square beyond was buzzing with activity, with many from South Concordia taking advantage of the occasion to shop for goods not readily available at their much smaller market. Kimura Clothiers and Devereaux's were certain to be crowded today, though Darius imagined that every store would see a boost in traffic. Certainly, none of the owners were going to be present for the dedication ceremonies. This was a mild disappointment, though he could not fault Saika, Frank, or any of the others for tending to their businesses.

On the bright side, the weather was cooperating. What had been a cool, overcast morning melted away as Bravo rose from its slumber. Patchwork tufts of fluffy clouds drifted lazily in the sky. Gentle breezes kicked up every few minutes, carrying with them the scents of home: floral shrubs, baking bread, and the occasional whiff of fertilizer from the farms. On top of that, the pungent smell of barbecue and wood smoke lingered.

I couldn't have asked for a better Unification Day.

It was Concordia's fourth official birthday. The anniversary milestone was one celebrated throughout the colony, and as each year passed, its importance grew more profound. It was a day of hope for the future, and remembrance of those who sacrificed their lives for the stability of Concordia. Yet for Darius, the bigger achievement was a year without a crisis. In retrospect he couldn't see anything different with how he ran things, but the time had flown by quickly, and a realization finally began to sink in.

Looks like we've finally turned the corner, Darius thought as he looked out at the gathered crowd. New parents cradled their babies in their arms and hoisted toddlers onto their shoulders. He could easily pick out a dozen children who had not even been conceived when the ships touched down. They were the first generation of native Concordians.

Darius nodded to Deputy Governor Dayton, who let loose an ear-splitting whistle. The chaotic din of the crowd quickly subsided as attention fell on Darius. He could still hear the distant commotion of commerce from the market square, though his audience was silent and rapt. He stepped onto a park bench just off the road.

"Welcome, my friends," he began, projecting his voice so all could hear. "I know that a lot of you got up early to take the long walk here from South Concordia, and we are very pleased to host you on this Unification Day. There are precious few occasions each year when the people of our community can come together to rest, reflect, and celebrate such a momentous point in our brief history."

The unilateral attention that he received harkened back to another time, just after the formation of the colony. The only other time so many people had hung on his every word: the day that he was elected as governor. It made him suddenly self-conscious, and he looked away shyly, as if he wasn't worthy. As if he was some remnant from the dead planet more than four light-years away. His fingers trembled for a moment, and he reached for the pocket that held his speech notes. But he stopped.

"We've had many trials in the first four years of our existence," he continued. "Before we left Earth, I had often heard comparisons of our mission to that of westward expansion and settlement in the nineteenth century. We've all seen firsthand the kind the kind of heartbreak and suffering that those early pioneers did. Our second winter on Demeter was darkened by the loss of loved friends, family, and neighbors. We felt the pangs of starvation as a people. Our young town has felt the burning rage of discontent and the soul shredding anguish of death. But unlike the pioneers of the West, we cannot go home when things get tough."

Darius took a moment to gather himself. He smiled as his eyes reconnected with the crowd, the anxiety melting away. His identity as Concordian was no longer in doubt. He was the leader of his people. He had starved with them and bled with them. Wept with them and laughed with them. And together they had achieved something truly incredible in such a short time.

"Nor did the thought ever cross our mind. This is our home." He swept one hand across the crowd. "This is family. My family and yours. We thrive by helping each other every day in Unity and Honor. And it is because of that we've grown faster than we could have thought possible. It is my hope that, with our bright future dawning, we can enjoy many more days to come. It is in that spirit that I dedicate our first public park."

Darius turned around and opened his arms, inviting the crowd to take in the beautiful sights beyond. Lush green grass carpeted the short, rolling hills from Foundation Street all the way to *Michael's* hull. A ten foot tall statue of stone and bronze sat twenty feet from him, surrounded by benches, flower shrubs, and a crisply maintained dirt path that radiated out in spokes from the monument. Deeper into the park, open fields gave way to rows of neatly spaced saplings of a dozen varieties, both native hardwoods and Earth fruit trees. The promenade created by the arbors extended out of sight behind the Civic Hall. Wisps of smoke rose from the promenade, and he could see the white mess hall tents ready to receive a couple thousand hungry celebrants. Pride swelled within him; he had been pleased with the project at every stage of its construction, and handing it over to the people was the ultimate culmination of that success.

He turned back to the people, who were still taking in the scope of their gift. He smiled. "I declare Benedict Square officially open, and invite you all to enjoy it. There will be food and drink for all throughout the day down at the Arbor Promenade, and tours of Civic Hall are available for those who are interested."

Darius stepped down and started to walk away to claps and cheers. But then he noticed confusion and apprehension among the people. A few timidly wandered out toward the park, but most stayed in the throng, chatting amongst each other.

He threw his arms up and down excitedly. "Come on, don't be shy! It's Unification Day! It's time to celebrate!"

The people's hesitation melted away, and Benedict Square instantly became the heart of festivity.

Spring had never been so warm. Not even the hot Texas sun had stirred Cal's blood as much as the combination of celebration, alcohol, and Alexis's radiant warmth as she snuggled close to him. The grass underneath them moderated the temperature somewhat, but only invigorated the romantic feelings burning within him. His passion was sure to boil over later in the evening once they finally made their way home.

Lively music from a guitar duet carried over the joyful squeals of children. Tantalizing smells of grilling food rolled in waves with every breeze, but he was so stuffed that the very thought of food threatened to make his stomach burst. Cal stretched his legs as much as he could without disturbing Alexis, though unsuccessfully, as she stirred and her eyes fluttered open.

"How long have I been out?" she yawned.

"Not long. Fifteen minutes, maybe."

She purred contentedly, closing her eyes again and resting her hand on his chest. "I don't want to move ever again."

He chuckled as he brushed her hair gently with his hand. "I promise I won't make you move until Darius kicks us out. Or I get hungry again. Whichever comes first."

"Good. That gives us two days, I'm guessing, based on how much you annihilated."

She's calling you fat, Jerk taunted, though his voice was very distant.

Months earlier, the end of winter signaled the availability of Dr. Taylor's anti-psychotic medication. Jerk was quickly silenced by the herbal concoction, though he still showed up whenever Cal drank. He could still be as big of a pain as ever, so Cal tried to keep his drinking to an absolute minimum, though this was a struggle in itself since launching his distilling business.

"What can I say?" he replied, ignoring the voice in his head. "Gail knows just what I like. And it's not like my wife is cooking. She sometimes puts me on these weird diets, or tries new and radical things."

Alexis playfully slapped him and giggled. "Oh, poor mistreated Cal. Wasting away without another woman to cook for him."

"There'll probably be something about that on my tombstone. Here lies Cal, starved to death by love. All he wanted was a Reaper burger."

Alexis smiled and repositioned so that her head was on his chest. "Glad you enjoyed it. And I'm so glad I didn't have to cook for all these people today."

Yeah, what a real white knight you are, Jerk prodded. *Having her peddle your liquor for you.*

"Oh, I forgot to ask you," he said. "How much vodka did we sell?"

"Well, get ready to bust your butt when we get home," she replied impishly. "All of it."

"All of it?" he gasped.

"Yep. Every bottle. Frank also placed a backorder for three more cases. He's got the empties ready for us to pick up whenever. He also gave me an order list for some soaps he needs."

Cal bolted upright, forcing a mild protest from Alexis. "He's never ordered that much from us before. Consigned, yes. But ordered?"

"He's got some big order in the works with Norris. Looks like this might become a regular thing."

He whooped with joy and squeezed her tight. "That's great news! That should put us even."

"Better than," she corrected. "We're finally in the black. Not by much, just a few favors, but still…"

Ooh, a few favors in the black. Don't spend it all in one place.

Shut up or I'll stop drinking again.

"It's what I've been waiting for. That means it's time," he said. His nerves started to jitter, but they could not stand against his elation.

"Time for what?"

He cupped her hands in his and looked deep into her emerald eyes. "Time to start our family."

Alexis's jaw dropped open in stunned silence, then she squealed and threw her arms around his neck.

Oh, you dumb son of a bitch, Jerk whined.

* * *

J.C. Rainier

Ruina Raphael

Chief James Vandemark
2 July, 5 yal, late afternoon
Camp Eight
>|

The storm curtain of the chief's hut parted suddenly, startling the family within.

"There's something going on, Chief," Troy stated nervously. "You better get out here."

James nodded and pardoned himself from the game of rummy he was playing with Jeanette and Kristin. He followed his trusted advisor outside. As they made their way to the vantage point at the edge of town that looked down on the shore, he noticed that the clouds had grown at least three shades darker. Distant thunder announced the arrival of another storm with its deep rumble. James scanned the choppy seas just offshore, as well as the white sands at the jungle's edge.

"Where's the fishing fleet?" he gasped. Not a single canoe or catamaran was to be found, not even on the shoreline.

"I don't know. I was patching up a loose panel on the clinic roof. One minute I look over and they're all out there, then I look again a couple minutes later and they're gone. All of them."

James closed his eyes, listening to the distant thunder and smelling the sea air. The wind was in his face, the tang of the salty air too sharp, the thunder too close. He snapped his eyes open.

"Get everyone to shelter, now!" he commanded.

"But what about the..."

James didn't give Troy the chance to finish. "Now!" he bellowed as he burst into a headlong sprint down the sea road.

Damn it. If the fishermen got caught, we don't have much time to prepare.

James felt the first warm drops of rain splash on his face as he bolted from the village. But his flight left him with a dilemma; should he head for the farmhouses to warn their occupants, or come to the aid of the fishing fleet? Either decision was equally heroic and damnable. His people were hanging on by the thinnest of threads, and losing either could mean starvation. He had nearly reached the fork in the road that would force a decision when he saw Nick Petrovsky stumble from the jungle near the beach.

"Nick! Nick, come here!" he shouted, competing with the wind.

Nick changed course, staggering to meet James at the fork in the sea road. His hair and clothes were dripping wet. The rain had just started on the island a minute earlier, leading James to believe that the fisherman had abandoned his canoe, or at least been thrown from it. Blood ran from a gash on his upper arm, flowing quickly down as the rain diluted it.

"What happened out there?" James asked, wrapping his arm around the fisherman to steady him.

Nick was still panting from his exertion when he spoke. "We thought the storm was going to skirt the island, just like the last one. But then it slowed down and took a turn right for us. Waves dumped us right over just before we got back to land. Our canoe broke apart. The waves were coming in fast, they threw us right on the beach. Part of the canoe landed on me."

"What about the others? What happened to them?" James was having a hard time shouting over the escalating wind.

"Mike's with Martin. They're trying to find any others that made it. We got caught with our pants down, Chief. The whole fleet's gone."

Shit.

The rain intensified dramatically, coming down in sheets that stung when they pelted exposed skin. Time was up. The storm had arrived, and his fishermen were still exposed.

"Get your ass back to the village. Take cover. Keep your dad safe," he ordered.

Nick didn't hesitate. The winds had intensified again, and standing upright was now a hazard. There was no way either of them was going to search for the wayward fishermen. James took a deep breath, and callously wrote off Michael and Martin as dead. There was only enough time left for James to find cover. The farms were the same distance from where he stood as the village was, so he sprinted toward the farms, hoping he could at least spare one more family by helping them secure their home.

Giant palms near the shore protected him from the wind long enough for the path to wind to the leeward side of the farm hill. Even still, the raging tempest buffeted everything. The protection that the hill's shoulder provided was limited, and twice he lost his footing and was forced to stay flat to the ground until the gust passed. James collected himself for the final push to the first farmhouse. His legs burned like hot irons were pressed against his calves and quads, but he pushed through.

Chief James Vandemark made it to within fifteen feet of the storm curtain, but his luck ended there. In his zeal to save as many lives as possible, he forgot that the slope changed at the last moment, exposing him to the windward side of the hill. Hurricane-force winds swept him off his feet and threw him into the sky like the insignificant speck of matter that he was.

He did, however, have plenty of time to think about his mortality and his family before crashing back to the ground, miles away, ending his life in an instant.

J.C. Rainier

William Vandemark
6 July, 5 yal, early evening
Colonial cemetery, 1 mile inland from Camp Eight
>|

Will didn't think it possible to remain calm under these circumstances. Though his soul has been torn asunder and his mind screamed in torment, his body gave only the slightest clues to his pain. A single tear rolled down his cheek, and his knuckles drained of color from the death grip he had on the shovel. He pointed the tip into the ground and leaned on it. His younger sister, Kris, fell to her knees, wailing.

Each metallic rasp as Daniel's shovel sunk into dirt left Will even emptier. His sister no doubt felt the same anguish, watching their mother's broken body slowly covered with dirt in her shallow grave. They never found their father's body. It didn't matter. Everyone knew he was dead after Nick told his story when the hurricane passed.

Each of the thirty-five survivors had a story to tell. Most were the same; confusion, followed by utter terror when they realized how severe the storm actually was, capped off with laments for the dead. Like most stories told during Camp Eight's tragic history, they were largely tales of suffering and death. Only one story of sacrifice and heroics had been told, but even that came with an unbearable price tag.

Will glanced to his right, catching sight of Gina and Karina. Each held a toddler in their arms; Gina clutched her half-sister Daphne, and Karina held Diego Serrano. Gabi's half-brother looked around with wide, curious eyes, occasionally pointing at something and commenting in butchered, barely coherent words. Neither of the children should have been alive, but for that one sacrifice. It was also a minor miracle that the survivors were able to hear the story. It was told by Aidan Brennan, an orphaned child who almost never spoke.

The villagers of Camp Eight were no strangers to storms. The tropical island was regularly drenched by vigorous downpours, and occasionally was subject to high winds, which was the reason storm curtains were developed to begin with. But the weather experts—in this case fishermen, since the village lacked any sort of scientific methods or tools—noted that they expected the storm to pass offshore. Just another in a series of storms narrowly missing the island, which was also not unusual.

But they had been wrong about both the intensity and direction of the storm. It slowed and hooked, hitting the island with all its fury. Camp Eight had almost no warning. Troy Bryant ran from dwelling to dwelling, shouting about the incoming storm. He barely had enough time to get to the Palm Palace in time to secure it. Aidan was inside, along with the two young children, Charlotte Bryant, and two more children who perished in the storm. It was Aidan who told the survivors about how Troy and the other children were sucked through the roof of the place when it peeled back like a cheap can, and how Charlotte forced the children into the corner, clutching each of them for dear life.

Charlotte was discovered the next day, still shielding the children long after a blow to the head had sapped the life from her body. Aidan was able to use his own body to keep her corpse from crushing and suffocating the younger children.

Will wiped the tear from his eye and placed his hand on Kris's shoulder, though she was inconsolable. Daniel drove a crude wooden cross into the ground, marking the completed grave.

Goodbye, Mom. He thought. More tears welled up, and his throat tightened.

The last grave had been filled. The last body buried. Will picked his sister up off the ground, urging her to go to the others. She screamed and protested at first, but eventually stumbled off, crying the whole way. He walked slowly behind her. He did not look at her, but instead at the grave markers that he passed, noting the names of dear friends and village elders who were gone.

Dr. Ken Petrovsky. Charlotte and Troy Bryant. Mark and Emilia Reiber. Leight. Jenkins. Captain Kimura. He clenched his teeth together. *Anyone and everyone who has ever had a hand in leading this God-forsaken colony. They're dead. We've failed.*

He reached the group to find Gina and Karina consoling his sister. The rest looked at him expectantly.

"What?" he growled in irritation. "It's over. Time to go."

"Go where?" Gabi asked.

"Home," he retorted as he brushed past her. Daniel caught his arm and stopped him.

"What home? The town's gone, Will. We've been living in shells since the storm passed."

Will paused. He turned around, checking the expressions of the survivors once again. Fear, concern, and apprehension were written all over the faces of everyone old enough to understand. And they all looked to him. A sickening realization dawned on him, something he did not think of when he volunteered to coordinate search and rescue efforts immediately after the storm.

I'm the new leader. I'm the only leader. No one else is left.

The skill sets of those left was even more disheartening. Of the thirty-five people that survived the hurricane, only sixteen adults were left. And that count included Karina, who was not quite eighteen years old. They were homeless, nearly defenseless, and would be starving in a matter of days.

This is what this fucking island does to us. Squeezes us until we die. Well, here we are, about to die.

The grief he felt was pushed aside violently by a surge of rage and determination. He wasn't about to die, nor would he let anyone else. He and Gina still had their whole lives together. He would watch after Kris, Daphne, Gabi, and Diego. The others were as good as family too, at this point. Daniel, Nick, Karina and Caleb. Even troublesome Marya and her brother Aidan deserved better than to just wait for their deaths.

"We will survive," he said, focusing his determination as a plan formulated in his head. "We start little. The pod on the beach may be dead and on its side, but it will still do for a shelter. We move in tonight. Nick, you take Daniel and Caleb fishing tomorrow. Show them what to do. Kris and Marya will scavenge the town and its surroundings for anything we can use. Tools, food, containers. Anything at all. Gina will watch the kids. Gabi and I will hunt."

"What about boats?" Nick asked. "They've all been smashed and sunk by the storm."

"Any parts you can recover and reuse, drag onto the shore. We'll need them eventually. If we're not gathering food or building something, we need to be spending our time training and learning. No more wasted time. We eat, we sleep, we forage, and we train. We need to share our knowledge with each other now. If there's anything we need to know that we don't, tell me and we'll figure it out together. Building skills, survival skills, whatever helps us along."

"Just what are you saying?" Gina added, her voice apprehensive.

"I'm saying we stop letting this cursed island pick us off. Do you really think I want to wait around here and let some other disaster sweep us off the map entirely?"

Gabi smirked. "No way."

"Damn right, Gabs. I know this island better than anyone, and I still remember my dad talking about where the other ships were supposed to land."

"Other ships?" Daniel protested. "We don't even know if they landed. They could have blown up just like *Raphael*."

"They could have. We might leave here and find they never made it. But damn it, I'd rather die trying to do something to save ourselves than just wait around to die. And if I'm right, we'll have a city of four *thousand* people waiting for us. Strength in numbers. No more sorrows."

Something stirred within the group. He could see the wheels turning as they discussed Will's proposal. Gabi removed herself from the conversation, nodding at Will and taking a place by him.

"He's right," she chimed in. "We need to go somewhere else. Even if there's no city, anywhere else has got to be better than here. I'm going with him."

"Me too," Gina affirmed.

One after another, the adults and older children confirmed their willingness to try, though some did so grudgingly. In the end, only Nick and Daniel refrained from volunteering. Will wasn't about to let them stay behind and perish, so he declared an edict, forcing them to come along.

"We will need to work hard and fast," he reminded them. "We need to come up with a ship design that can carry us and our supplies across the sea, and be something that we can build with the materials we have. I'm guessing this will take more than one ship. We need to have all of them built and stocked before storm season next year. Let's go to the pod and get some sleep. It might be the last time any of us gets rest for a very long time."

>END PLAYBACK|

Credits and Acknowledgements
14 November 2013
The real Earth, somewhere in Washington State
>|

How time flies. It's approaching the holiday season, and it's time to release the fourth installment of Project Columbus. There's only one more book to go!

As always, I need to give special thanks to my beta readers Sarah and Karie. This particular title was approached from a different aspect from my previous works, and they helped guide my course to keep everything understandable to readers of the previous books. That's not to say that I didn't have fun bringing in the viewpoints of characters who previously had no Point of View reference.

I would like to profusely thank Mathew and Bridgette Reuther of Oakenbrand Press. They have taken me in under their wings and given me so much. Mathew continues to be a valuable source in the world of publishing. I am proud to have Bridgette's beautiful artwork gracing the cover of my book for the sixth time. Wait, what, J.C.? Sixth? That's right, she designed both the first and second edition covers of Flight and Ashes. That counts in my book. Or on my books, as the case may be. But there's more. Oakenbrand is now my official publishing house, and for that I am eternally thankful. I look forward to bringing many books to you, the reader, through this partnership.

Of course, continued thanks to my wife Megan and our three boys for putting up with my general grouchiness as I have tried to correlate the existing start to book 5 with what I have written here in *Winter*. One of these days I'm going to learn to stop breaking the space-time continuum. At least until I write a story that allows for said breaking.

Finally, many thanks to you, the readers, without whom I'm just some guy hammering a keyboard to death mercilessly without reason. If you've been with me since *Flight*, it is truly my honor to have you back, and I would love for you to stick around with me one more time, to the end. If you picked up this book on a Kindle promo without reading the first three books (it happens), I'm sorry for any confusion I caused. If the story was intriguing, I would invite you to go back to *Flight* and start from the beginning, even if you now know some spoilers.

Thanks once again, everyone, and I'll see you again in spring with the release of *Columbus: Mercy*.

About the Author:

J.C. Rainier is product of the Pacific Northwest, born in the Seattle area in 1978, and living in the Puget Sound area his whole life. He is the younger of two children in his family, and his older brother proved to be a giant pest up through his teenage years (as siblings tend to be).

J.C.'s parents were both educators working at the middle school level, and he married into another family of educators. In his family, counting in-laws, there are now two retired principals, two retired teachers, a retired school counselor, and an active science teacher.

In his youth, J.C. read quite a lot. The Call of the Wild was one of his early favorites, and into middle school he began to devour other books such as Anne McCaffrey's Dragonriders of Pern series. Unfortunately, J.C. developed a form of dylexia that made reading from the page of a book difficult. It was later discovered that the curvature of the page itself caused the issue, and the advent of the eReader (with its perfectly flat screen) has allowed him to once again enjoy reading as he used to.

He enjoys both indoor and outdoor pursuits including computers, cars, and camping. J.C. and his wife enjoy hockey, and set aside time several times each season to watch the local WHL franchise.

J.C. and his wife are raising three boys, including a set of twins. If his blog ever fails to make sense, he's probably had a very long night just prior to writing it. If said writing is just a random set of characters similar to "adsk,wr3.1", then one of the children has managed a surprise attack on his laptop.

. . .

www.ingramcontent.com/pod-product-compliance
Lightning Source LLC
Chambersburg PA
CBHW071919220626
47052CB00002B/425